WHERE SHE WENT

where
she
went

Gayle Forman

DUTTON BOOKS

An imprint of Penguin Group (USA) Inc.

DUTTON BOOKS

A member of Penguin Group (USA) Inc.

Published by the Penguin Group | Penguin Group (USA) Inc., 375 Hudson Street, New York, New York 10014, U.S.A. | Penguin Group (Canada), 90 Eglinton Avenue East, Suite 700, Toronto, Ontario M4P 2Y3, Canada (a division of Pearson Penguin Canada Inc.) | Penguin Books Ltd, 80 Strand, London WC2R 0RL, England | Penguin Ireland, 25 St Stephen's Green, Dublin 2, Ireland (a division of Penguin Books Ltd) | Penguin Group (Australia), 250 Camberwell Road, Camberwell, Victoria 3124, Australia (a division of Pearson Australia Group Pty Ltd) | Penguin Books India Pvt Ltd, 11 Community Centre, Panchsheel Park, New Delhi - 110 017, India | Penguin Group (NZ), 67 Apollo Drive, Rosedale, North Shore 0632, New Zealand (a division of Pearson New Zealand Ltd.) | Penguin Books (South Africa) (Pty) Ltd, 24 Sturdee Avenue, Rosebank, Johannesburg 2196, South Africa | Penguin Books Ltd, Registered Offices: 80 Strand, London WC2R 0RL, England

The publisher does not have any control over and does not assume any responsibility for author or third-party websites or their content.

Epigraph: Copyright © 1931, 1958 by Edna St. Vincent Millay and Norma Millay Ellis. Reprinted with permission of Elizabeth Barnett, The Millay Society.

Library of Congress Cataloging-in-Publication Data Forman, Gayle. Where she went / by Gayle Forman. — 1st ed. p. cm. Sequel to: If I stay. Summary: Adam, now a rising rock star, and Mia, a successful cellist, reunite in New York and reconnect after the horrific events that tore them apart when Mia almost died in a car accident three years earlier. ISBN 978-0-525-42294-5 (hardcover) [1. Interpersonal relations—Fiction. 2. Emotional problems—Fiction. 3. Rock music—Fiction. 4. Violoncello—Fiction. 5. New York (N.Y.)—Fiction.] I. Title. PZ7.F75876Wh 2011 [Fic]--dc22 2010013474

Published in the United States by Dutton Books, a member of Penguin Group (USA) Inc., 345 Hudson Street, New York, New York 10014 www.penguin.com/youngreaders

Designed by Abby Kuperstock
Printed in USA | First Edition | 10 9 8 7 6

FOR MY PARENTS:
for saying I can.

It well may be that in a difficult hour,
Pinned down by pain and moaning for release,
Or nagged by want past resolution's power,
I might be driven to sell your love for peace,
Or trade the memory of this night for food.
It well may be. I do not think I would.

Excerpt from "Love is not all:
it is not meat nor drink."

BY EDNA ST. VINCENT MILLAY

WHERE SHE WENT

Every morning I wake up and I tell myself this: *It's just one day, one twenty-four-hour period to get yourself through.* I don't know when exactly I started giving myself this daily pep talk—or why. It sounds like a twelve-step mantra and I'm not in Anything Anonymous, though to read some of the crap they write about me, you'd think I should be. I have the kind of life a lot of people would probably sell a kidney to just experience a bit of. But still, I find the need to remind myself of the temporariness of a day, to reassure myself that I got through yesterday, I'll get through today.

This morning, after my daily prodding, I glance at the minimalist digital clock on the hotel nightstand. It reads 11:47, positively crack-of-dawn for me. But the front desk has already rang with two wake-up calls, followed by a polite-but-firm buzz from our manager, Aldous. Today might be just one day, but it's packed.

I'm due at the studio to lay down a few final guitar tracks for some Internet-only version of the first single of our just-released album. Such a gimmick. Same song, new guitar track, some vocal effects, pay an extra buck for it. "These days, you've gotta milk a dollar out of every dime," the suits at the label are so fond of reminding us.

After the studio, I have a lunch interview with some reporter from *Shuffle*. Those two events are kinda like the bookends of what my life has become: making the music, which I like, and talking about making the music, which I loathe. But they're flip sides of the same coin. When Aldous calls a second time I finally kick off the duvet and grab the prescription bottle from the side table. It's some anti-anxiety thing I'm supposed to take when I'm feeling jittery.

Jittery is how I normally feel. Jittery I've gotten used to. But ever since we kicked off our tour with three shows at Madison Square Garden, I've been feeling something else. Like I'm about to be sucked into something powerful and painful. Vortexy.

Is that even a word? I ask myself.

You're talking to yourself, so who the hell cares? I reply, popping a couple of pills. I pull on some boxers, and go to the door of my room, where a pot of coffee is already waiting. It's been left there by a hotel employee, undoubtedly under strict instructions to stay out of my way.

I finish my coffee, get dressed, and make my way down the service elevator and out the side entrance—the guest-relations manager has kindly provided me with special access keys so I can avoid the scenester parade in the lobby. Out on the sidewalk, I'm greeted by a blast of steaming New York air. It's kind of oppressive, but I like that the air is wet. It reminds me of Oregon, where the rain falls endlessly, and even on the hottest of summer days, blooming white cumulus clouds float above, their shadows reminding you that summer's heat is fleeting, and the rain's never far off.

In Los Angeles, where I live now, it hardly ever rains. And the heat, it's never-ending. But it's a dry heat. People there use this aridness as a blanket excuse for all of the hot, smoggy city's excesses. "It may be a hundred and seven degrees today," they'll brag, "but at least it's a dry heat."

But New York is a wet heat; by the time I reach the studio ten blocks away on a desolate stretch in the West

Fifties, my hair, which I keep hidden under a cap, is damp. I pull a cigarette from my pocket and my hand shakes as I light up. I've had a slight tremor for the last year or so. After extensive medical checks, the doctors declared it nothing more than nerves and advised me to try yoga.

When I get to the studio, Aldous is waiting outside under the awning. He looks at me, at my cigarette, back at my face. I can tell by the way that he's eyeballing me, he's trying to decide whether he needs to be Good Cop or Bad Cop. I must look like shit because he opts for Good Cop.

"Good morning, Sunshine," he says jovially.

"Yeah? What's ever good about morning?" I try to make it sound like a joke.

"Technically, it's afternoon now. We're running late."

I stub out my cigarette. Aldous puts a giant paw on my shoulder, incongruously gentle. "We just want one guitar track on 'Sugar,' just to give it that little something extra so fans buy it all over again." He laughs, shakes his head at what the business has become. "Then you have lunch with *Shuffle,* and we have a photo shoot for that Fashion Rocks thing for the *Times* with the rest of the band around five, and then a quick drinks thing with some money guys at the label, and then I'm off to the airport. Tomorrow, you have a quick little meeting with publicity and merchandising. Just smile and don't say a lot. After that you're on your lonesome until London."

On my lonesome? As opposed to being in the warm bosom of family when we're all together? I say. Only I say it to myself. More and more lately it seems as though the majority of my conversations are with myself. Given half the stuff I think, that's probably a good thing.

But this time I really will be by myself. Aldous and the rest of the band are flying to England tonight. I was supposed to be on the same flight as them until I realized that today was Friday the thirteenth, and I was like no fucking way! I'm dreading this tour enough as is, so I'm not jinxing it further by leaving on the official day of bad luck. So I'd had Aldous book me a day later. We're shooting a video in London and then doing a bunch of press before we start the European leg of our tour, so it's not like I'm missing a show, just a preliminary meeting with our video director. I don't need to hear about his artistic vision. When we start shooting, I'll do what he tells me.

I follow Aldous into the studio and enter a sound-proof booth where it's just me and a row of guitars. On the other side of the glass sit our producer, Stim, and the sound engineers. Aldous joins them. "Okay, Adam," says Stim, "one more track on the bridge and the chorus. Just to make that hook that much more sticky. We'll play with the vocals in the mixing."

"Hooky. Sticky. Got it." I put on my headphones and pick up my guitar to tune up and warm up. I try not to notice that in spite of what Aldous said a few minutes ago, it feels like I'm *already* all on my lonesome. Me alone in a soundproof booth. *Don't overthink it*, I tell myself. *This is how you record in a technologically advanced studio.* The only problem is, I felt the same way a few nights ago at the Garden. Up onstage, in front of eighteen thousand fans, alongside the people who, once upon a time, were part of my family, I felt as alone as I do in this booth.

Still, it could be worse. I start to play and my fingers nimble up and I get off the stool and bang and crank against my guitar, pummel it until it screeches and screams just the way I want it to. Or almost the way I want it to. There's probably a hundred grand's worth of guitars in this room, but none of them sound as good as my old Les Paul Junior—the guitar I'd had for ages, the one I'd recorded our first albums on, the one that, in a fit of stupidity or hubris or whatever, I'd allowed to be auctioned off for charity. The shiny, expensive replacements have never sounded or felt quite right. Still, when I crank it up loud, I do manage to lose myself for a second or two.

But it's over all too soon, and then Stim and the engineers are shaking my hand and wishing me luck on tour, and Aldous is shepherding me out the door and into a town car and we're whizzing down Ninth Avenue to SoHo, to a hotel whose restaurant the publicists from our record label have decided is a good spot for our interview. What, do they think I'm less likely to rant or say something alienating if I'm in an expensive public place? I remember back in the very early days, when the interviewers wrote 'zines or blogs and were fans and mostly wanted to rock-talk—to discuss the *music*—and they wanted to speak to all of us together. More often than not, it just turned into a normal conversation with everyone shouting their opinions over one another. Back then I never worried about guarding my words. But now the reporters interrogate me and the band separately, as though they're cops and they have me and my accomplices in adjacent cells and are trying to get us to implicate one another.

I need a cigarette before we go in, so Aldous and I stand outside the hotel in the blinding midday sun as a crowd of people gathers and checks me out while pretending not to. That's the difference between New York and the rest of the world. People are just as celebrity-crazed as anywhere, but New Yorkers—or at least the ones who consider themselves sophisticates and loiter along the kind of SoHo block I'm standing on now—put on this pretense that they don't care, even as they stare out from their three-hundred-dollar shades. Then they act all disdainful when out-of-towners break the code by rushing up and asking for an autograph as a pair of girls in U Michigan sweatshirts have just done, much to the annoyance of the nearby trio of snobs, who watch the girls and roll their eyes and give me a look of sympathy. As if the *girls* are the problem.

"We need to get you a better disguise, Wilde Man," Aldous says, after the girls, giggling with excitement, flutter away. He's the only one who's allowed to call me that anymore. Before it used to be a general nickname, a takeoff on my last name, Wilde. But once I sort of trashed a hotel room and after that "Wilde Man" became an unshakable tabloid moniker.

Then, as if on cue, a photographer shows up. You can't stand in front of a high-end hotel for more than three minutes before that happens. "Adam! Bryn inside?" A photo of me and Bryn is worth about quadruple one of me alone. But after the first flash goes off, Aldous shoves one hand in front of the guy's lens, and another in front of my face.

As he ushers me inside, he preps me. "The reporter is named Vanessa LeGrande. She's not one of those grizzled types you hate. She's young. Not younger than you, but early twenties, I think. Used to write for a blog before she got tapped by *Shuffle*."

"Which blog?" I interrupt. Aldous rarely gives me detailed rundowns on reporters unless there's a reason.

"Not sure. Maybe Gabber."

"Oh, Al, that's a piece-of-crap gossip site."

"*Shuffle* isn't a gossip site. And this is the cover exclusive."

"Fine. Whatever," I say, pushing through the restaurant doors. Inside it's all low steel-and-glass tables and leather banquettes, like a million other places I've been to. These restaurants think so highly of themselves, but really they're just overpriced, overstylized versions of McDonald's.

"There she is, corner table, the blonde with the streaks," Aldous says. "She's a sweet little number. Not that you have a shortage of sweet little numbers. Shit, don't tell Bryn I said that. Okay, forget it. I'll be up here at the bar."

Aldous staying for the interview? That's a publicist's job, except that I refused to be chaperoned by publicists. I must really seem off-kilter. "You babysitting?" I ask.

"Nope. Just thought you could use some backup."

Vanessa LeGrande is cute. Or maybe *hot* is a more accurate term. It doesn't matter. I can tell by the way she licks her lips and tosses her hair back that she knows it, and that pretty much ruins the effect. A tattoo of a snake runs up her wrist, and I'd bet our platinum album that she has a tramp stamp. Sure enough, when she reaches into her bag for her digital recorder, peeping up from the top of her low-slung jeans is a small inked arrow pointing south. *Classy.*

"Hey, Adam," Vanessa says, looking at me conspiratorially, like we're old buddies. "Can I just say I'm a huge fan? *Collateral Damage* got me through a devastating breakup senior year of college. So, thank you." She smiles at me.

"Uh, you're welcome."

"And now I'd like to return the favor by writing the best damn profile of Shooting Star ever to hit the page. So how about we get down to brass tacks and blow this thing right out of the water?"

Get down to brass tacks? Do people even understand half the crap that comes spilling out of their mouths? Vanessa may be attempting to be brassy or sassy or trying to win me over with candor or show me how real she is, but whatever it is she's selling, I'm not buying. "Sure," is all I say.

A waiter comes to take our order. Vanessa orders a salad; I order a beer. Vanessa flips through a Moleskine notebook. "I know we're supposed to be talking about *BloodSuckerSunshine* . . ." she begins.

Immediately, I frown. That's *exactly* what we're supposed to be talking about. That's why I'm here. Not to be friends. Not to swap secrets, but because it's part of my job to promote Shooting Star's albums.

Vanessa turns on her siren. "I've been listening to it for weeks, and I'm a fickle, hard-to-please girl." She laughs. In the distance, I hear Aldous clear his throat. I look at him. He's wearing a giant fake smile and giving me a thumbs-up. He looks ludicrous. I turn to Vanessa and force myself to smile back. "But now that your second major-label album is out and your harder sound is, I think we can all agree, established, I'm wanting to write a definitive survey. To chart your evolution from emo-core band to the scions of agita-rock."

Scions of agita-rock? This self-important wankjob deconstructionist crap was something that really threw me in the beginning. As far as I was concerned, I wrote songs: chords and beats and lyrics, verses and bridges and hooks. But then, as we got bigger, people began to dissect the songs, like a frog from biology class until there was nothing left but guts—tiny parts, so much less than the sum.

I roll my eyes slightly, but Vanessa's focused on her notes. "I was listening to some bootlegs of your really early stuff. It's so poppy, almost sweet comparatively. And I've been reading everything ever written about you guys, every blog post, every 'zine article. And almost everyone refers to this so-called Shooting Star "black hole," but no one really ever penetrates it. You have your little indie release; it does well; you were poised for the big leagues, but then this lag. Rumors were that you'd broken up. And then comes *Collateral Damage*. And pow." Vanessa mimes an explosion coming out of her closed fists.

It's a dramatic gesture, but not entirely off base. *Collateral Damage* came out two years ago, and within a month of its release, the single "Animate" had broken onto the national charts and gone viral. We used to joke you couldn't listen to the radio for longer than an hour without hearing it. Then "Bridge" catapulted onto the charts, and soon after the entire album was climbing to the number-one album slot on iTunes, which in turn made every Walmart in the country stock it, and soon it was bumping Lady Gaga off the number-one spot on the *Billboard* charts. For a while it seemed like the album was loaded onto the iPod of every person between the ages of twelve and twenty-four. Within a matter of months, our half-forgotten Oregon band was on the cover of *Time* magazine being touted as "The Millennials' Nirvana."

But none of this is news. It had all been documented, over and over again, ad nauseam, including in *Shuffle*. I'm not sure where Vanessa is going with it.

"You know, everyone seems to attribute the harder sound to the fact that Gus Allen produced *Collateral Damage*."

"Right," I say. "Gus likes to rock."

Vanessa takes a sip of water. I can hear her tongue ring click. "But Gus didn't write those lyrics, which are the foundation for all that oomph. You did. All that raw power and emotion. It's like *Collateral Damage* is the angriest album of the decade."

"And to think, we were going for the happiest."

Vanessa looks up at me, narrows her eyes. "I meant it as a compliment. It was very cathartic for a lot of people, myself included. And that's my point. Everyone knows something went down during your 'black hole.' It's going to come out eventually, so why not control the message? Who does the 'collateral damage' refer to?" she asks, making air quotes. "What happened with you guys? With you?"

Our waiter delivers Vanessa's salad. I order a second beer and don't answer her question. I don't say anything, just keep my eyes cast downward. Because Vanessa's right about one thing. We *do* control the message. In the early days, we got asked this question all the time, but we just kept the answers vague: took a while to find our sound, to write our songs. But now the band's big enough that our publicists issue a list of no-go topics to reporters: Liz and Sarah's relationship, mine and Bryn's, Mike's former drug problems—and the Shooting Star's "black hole." But Vanessa apparently didn't get the memo. I glance over at Aldous for some help, but he's in deep conversation with the bartender. So much for backup.

"The title refers to war," I say. "We've explained that before."

"Right," she says, rolling her eyes. "Because your lyrics are *so* political."

Vanessa stares at me with those big baby blues. This is a reporter's technique: create an awkward silence and wait for your subject to fill it in with babble. It won't work with me, though. I can outstare anyone.

Vanessa's eyes suddenly go cold and hard. She abruptly puts her breezy, flirty personality on the back burner and stares at me with hard ambition. She looks hungry, but it's an improvement because at least she's being herself. "What happened, Adam? I know there's a story there, *the* story of Shooting Star, and I'm going to be the one to tell it. What turned this indie-pop band into a primal rock phenomenon?"

I feel a cold hard fist in my stomach. "Life happened. And it took us a while to write the new stuff—"

"Took *you* a while," Vanessa interrupts. "You wrote both the recent albums."

I just shrug.

"Come on, Adam! *Collateral Damage* is your record. It's a masterpiece. You should be proud of it. And I just know the story behind it, behind your band, is your story, too. A huge shift like this, from collaborative indie quartet to star-driven emotional punk powerhouse—it's all on you. I mean you alone were the one up at the Grammys accepting the award for Best Song. What did that feel like?"

Like shit. "In case you forgot, the whole band won Best New Artist. And that was more than a year ago."

She nods. "Look, I'm not trying to diss anybody or reopen wounds. I'm just trying to understand the shift. In sound. In lyrics. In band dynamics." She gives me a knowing look. "All signs point to you being the catalyst."

"There's no catalyst. We just tinkered with our sound. Happens all the time. Like Dylan going electric. Like Liz Phair going commercial. But people tend to freak out when something diverges from their expectations."

"I just know there's something more to it," Vanessa continues, pushing forward against the table so hard that it shoves into my gut and I have to physically push it back.

"Well, you've obviously got your theory, so don't let the truth get in the way."

Her eyes flash for a quick second and I think I've pissed her off, but then she puts her hands up. Her nails are bitten down. "Actually, you want to know my theory?" she drawls.

Not particularly. "Lay it on me."

"I talked to some people you went to high school with."

I feel my entire body freeze up, soft matter hardening into lead. It takes extreme concentration to lift the glass to my lips and pretend to take a sip.

"I didn't realize that you went to the same high school as Mia Hall," she says lightly. "You know her? The cellist? She's starting to get a lot of buzz in that world. Or whatever the equivalent of buzz is in classical music. Perhaps hum."

The glass shakes in my hand. I have to use my other hand to help lower it to the table to keep from spilling all over myself. *All the people who really know what actually had happened back then aren't talking,* I remind myself. *Rumors, even true ones, are like flames: Stifle the oxygen and they sputter and die.*

"Our high school had a good arts program. It was kind of a breeding ground for musicians," I explain.

"That makes sense," Vanessa says, nodding. "There's a vague rumor that you and Mia were a couple in high school. Which was funny because I'd never read about it anywhere and it certainly seems noteworthy."

An image of Mia flashes before my eyes. Seventeen years old, those dark eyes full of love, intensity, fear, music, sex, magic, grief. Her freezing hands. My own freezing hands, now still grasping the glass of ice water.

"It would be noteworthy if it were true," I say, forcing my voice into an even tone. I take another gulp of water and signal the waiter for another beer. It's my third, the dessert course of my liquid lunch.

"So it's not?" She sounds skeptical.

"Wishful thinking," I reply. "We knew each other casually from school."

"Yeah, I couldn't get anyone who really knew either of you to corroborate it. But then I got a hold of an old yearbook and there's a sweet shot of the two of you. You look pretty coupley. The thing is, there's no name with the photo, just a caption. So unless you know what Mia looks like, you might miss it."

Thank you, Kim Schein: Mia's best friend, yearbook queen, paparazzo. We hadn't wanted that picture used, but Kim had snuck it in by not listing our names with it, just that stupid nickname.

"Groovy and the Geek?" Vanessa asks. "You guys even had a handle."

"You're using high school yearbooks as your source? What next? Wikipedia?"

"You're hardly a reliable source. You said you knew each other 'casually.'"

"Look, the truth is we maybe hooked up for a few weeks, right when those pictures got taken. But, hey, I dated a lot of girls in high school." I give her my best playboy smirk.

"So you haven't seen her since school then?"

"Not since she left for college," I say. That part, at least, is true.

"So how come when I interviewed the rest of your bandmates, they went all no comment when I asked about her?" she asks, eyeing me hard.

Because whatever else has gone wrong with us, we're still loyal. About that. I force myself to speak out loud: "Because there's nothing to tell. I think people like you like the sitcom aspect of, you know, two well-known musicians from the same high school being a couple."

"People like me?" Vanessa asks.

Vultures. Bloodsuckers. Soul-stealers. "Reporters," I say. "You're fond of fairy tales."

"Well, who isn't?" Vanessa says. "Although that woman's life has been anything but a fairy tale. She lost her whole family in a car crash."

Vanessa mock shudders the way you do when you talk about someone's misfortunes that have nothing to do with you, that don't touch you, and never will. I've never hit a woman in my life, but for one minute I want to punch her in the face, give her a taste of the pain she's so casually describing. But I hold it together and she carries on, clueless. "Speaking of fairy tales, are you and Bryn Shraeder having a baby? I keep seeing her in all the tabloids' bump watches."

"No," I reply. "Not that I know of." I'm damn sure Vanessa knows that Bryn is off-limits, but if talking about Bryn's supposed pregnancy will distract her, then I'll do it.

"*Not that you know of*? You're still together, right?"

God, the hunger in her eyes. For all her talk of writing definitive surveys, for all her investigative skills, she's no different from all the other hack journalists and stalker photographers, dying to be the first to deliver a big scoop, either on a birth: *Is It Twins for Adam and Bryn?* Or a death: *Bryn Tells Her Wilde Man: "It's Quits!"* Neither story is true, but some weeks I see both of them on the covers of different gossip rags at the same time.

I think of the house in L.A. that Bryn and I share. Or coinhabit. I can't remember the last time the two of us were there together at the same time for more than a week. She makes two, three films a year, and she just started her own production company. So between shooting and promoting her films and chasing down properties to produce, and me being in the studio and on tour, we seem to be on opposing schedules.

"Yep, Bryn and I are still together," I tell Vanessa. "And she's not pregnant. She's just into those peasant tops these days, so everyone always assumes it's to hide a belly. It's not."

Truth be told, I sometimes wonder if Bryn wears those tops on purpose, to court the bump watch as a way to tempt fate. She *seriously* wants a kid. Even though publicly, Bryn is twenty-four, in reality, she's twenty-eight and she claims her clock is ticking and all that. But I'm twenty-one, and Bryn and I have only been together a year. And I don't care if Bryn says that I have an old soul and have been through a lifetime already. Even if I were forty-one, and Bryn and I had just celebrated twenty years together, I wouldn't want a kid with her.

"Will she be joining you on the tour?"

At the mere mention of the tour, I feel my throat start to close up. The tour is sixty-seven nights long. *Sixty-seven.* I mentally pat for my pill bottle, grow calmer knowing it's there, but am smarter than to sneak one in front of Vanessa.

"Huh?" I ask.

"Is Bryn going to come meet you on the tour at all?"

I imagine Bryn on tour, with her stylists, her Pilates instructors, her latest raw-foods diet. "Maybe."

"How do you like living in Los Angeles?" Vanessa asks. "You don't seem like the SoCal type."

"It's a dry heat," I reply.

"What?"

"Nothing. A joke."

"Oh. Right." Vanessa eyes me skeptically. I no longer read interviews about myself, but when I used to, words like *inscrutable* were often used. And *arrogant*. Is that really how people see me?

Thankfully, our allotted hour is up. She closes her notebook and calls for the check. I catch Aldous's relieved-looking eyes to let him know we're wrapping up.

"It was nice meeting you, Adam," she says.

"Yeah, you too," I lie.

"I gotta say, you're a puzzle." She smiles and her teeth gleam an unnatural white. "But I like puzzles. Like your lyrics, all those grisly images on *Collateral Damage*. And the lyrics on the new record, also very cryptic. You know some critics question whether *Blood-*

SuckerSunshine can match the intensity of *Collateral Damage.* . . ."

I know what's coming. I've heard this before. It's this thing that reporters do. Reference other critics' opinions as a backhanded way to espouse their own. And I know what she's *really* asking, even if she doesn't: *How does it feel that the only worthy thing you ever created came from the worst kind of loss?*

Suddenly, it's all too much. Bryn and the bump watch. Vanessa with my high school yearbook. The idea that nothing's sacred. Everything's fodder. That my life belongs to anyone but me. Sixty-seven nights. *Sixty-seven, sixty-seven.* I push the table hard so that glasses of water and beer go clattering into her lap.

"What the—?"

"This interview's over," I growl.

"I know that. Why are you freaking out on me?"

"Because you're nothing but a vulture! This has fuck all to do with music. It's about picking everything apart."

Vanessa's eyes dance as she fumbles for her recorder. Before she has a chance to turn it back on, I pick it up and slam it against the table, shattering it, and then dump it into a glass of water for good measure. My hand is shaking and my heart is pounding and I feel the beginnings of a panic attack, the kind that makes me sure I'm about to die.

"What did you just do?" Vanessa screams. "I don't have a backup."

"Good."

"How am I supposed to write my article now?"

"You call *that* an article?"

"Yeah. Some of us have to work for a living, you prissy, temperamental ass—"

"Adam!" Aldous is at my side, laying a trio of hundred-dollar bills on the table. "For a new one," he says to Vanessa, before ushering me out of the restaurant and into a taxi. He throws another hundred-dollar bill at the driver after he balks at my lighting up. Aldous reaches into my pocket and grabs my prescription bottle, shakes a tablet into his hand, and says, "Open up," like some bearish mother.

He waits until we're a few blocks from my hotel, until I've sucked down two cigarettes in one continuous inhale and popped another anxiety pill. "What happened back there?"

I tell him. Her questions about the "black hole." Bryn. Mia.

"Don't worry. We can call *Shuffle*. Threaten to pull their exclusive if they don't put a different reporter on

the piece. And maybe this gets into the tabloids or Gabber for a few days, but it's not much of a story. It'll blow
over."

Aldous is saying all this stuff calmly, like, *hey, it's only
rock 'n' roll,* but I can read the worry in his eyes.

"I can't, Aldous."

"Don't worry about it. You don't have to. It's just an
article. It'll be handled."

"Not just that. I can't do it. Any of it."

Aldous, who I don't think has slept a full night since
he toured with Aerosmith, allows himself to look exhausted for a few seconds. Then he goes back to manager mode. "You've just got pretour burnout. Happens
to the best of 'em," he assures me. "Once you get on
the road, in front of the crowds, start to feel the love,
the adrenaline, the music, you'll be energized. I mean,
hell, you'll be fried for sure, but happy-fried. And come
November, when this is over, you can go veg out on an
island somewhere where nobody knows who you are,
where nobody gives a shit about Shooting Star. Or wild
Adam Wilde."

November? It's August now. That's three months.
And the tour is sixty-seven nights. *Sixty-seven.* I repeat
it in my head like a mantra, except it does the opposite
of what a mantra's supposed to do. It makes me want to
grab fistfuls of my hair and yank.

And how do I tell Aldous, how do I tell any of them, that the music, the adrenaline, *the love*, all the things that mitigate how hard this has become, all of that's gone? All that's left is this vortex. And I'm right on the edge of it.

My entire body is shaking. I'm losing it. A day might be just twenty-four hours but sometimes getting through just one seems as impossible as scaling Everest.

TWO

Needle and thread, flesh and bone
Spit and sinew, heartbreak is home
Your suture lines sparkle like diamonds
Bright stars to light my confinement

"STITCH"
COLLATERAL DAMAGE, TRACK 7

Aldous leaves me in front of my hotel. "Look, man, I think you just need some time to chill. So, listen: I'm gonna clear the schedule for the rest of the day and cancel your meetings tomorrow. Your flight to London's not till seven; you don't have to be at the airport till five." He glances at his phone. "That's more than twenty-four hours to do whatever you want to. I promise you, you'll feel so much better. Just go be free."

Aldous is peering at me with a look of calculated concern. He's my friend, but I'm also his responsibility. "I'm gonna change my flight," he announces. "I'll fly with you tomorrow."

I'm embarrassed by how grateful I am. Flying Upper Class with the band is no great shakes. We all tend to stay plugged into our own luxury pods, but at least when I fly with them, I'm not alone. When I fly alone, who knows who I'll be seated next to? I once had a Japanese businessman who didn't stop talking to me at all during a ten-hour flight. I'd wanted to be moved but hadn't wanted to seem like the kind of rock-star prick who'd ask to be moved, so I'd sat there, nodding my head, not understanding half of what he was saying. But worse yet are the times when I'm truly alone for those long-haul flights.

I know Aldous has lots to do in London. More to the point, missing tomorrow's meeting with the rest of the band and the video director will be one more little earthquake. But whatever. There are too many fault lines to count now. Besides, nobody blames Aldous; they blame me.

So, it's a huge imposition to let Aldous spend an extra day in New York. But I still accept his offer, even as I downplay his generosity by muttering, "Okay."

"Cool. You clear your head. I'll leave you alone, won't even call. Want me to pick you up here or meet you at the airport?" The rest of the band is staying downtown.

We've gotten into the habit of staying in separate hotels since the last tour, and Aldous diplomatically alternates between staying at my hotel and theirs. This time he's with them.

"Airport. I'll meet you in the lounge," I tell him.

"Okay then. I'll order you a car for four. Until then, just chill." He gives me a half handshake, half hug and then he's back inside the cab, zooming off to his next order of business, probably mending the fences that I've thrashed today.

I go around to the service entrance and make my way to my hotel room. I take a shower, ponder going back to sleep. But these days, sleep eludes me even with a medicine cabinet full of psychopharmacological assistance. From the eighteenth-story windows, I can see the afternoon sun bathing the city in a warm glow, making New York feel cozy somehow, but making the suite feel claustrophobic and hot. I throw on a clean pair of jeans and my lucky black T-shirt. I wanted to reserve this shirt for tomorrow when I leave for the tour, but I feel like I need some luck right now, so it's gonna have to pull double duty.

I turn on my iPhone. There are fifty-nine new email messages and seventeen new voice mails, including several from the label's now-certainly irate publicist and a bunch from Bryn, asking how it went in the studio and with the interview. I could call her, but what's the point? If I tell her about Vanessa LeGrande, she'll get all upset with me for losing my "public face" in front of a reporter. She's trying to train me out of that bad habit. She says every time I lose it in front of the press, I only whet their appetites for more. "Give them a dull public face, Adam, and they'll stop writing so much about you," she constantly advises me. The thing is, I have a feeling if I told Bryn which question set me off, she'd probably lose her public face, too.

I think about what Aldous said about getting away from it all, and I turn off the phone and toss it on the nightstand. Then I grab my hat, shades, my pills, and wallet and am out the door. I turn up Columbus, making my way toward Central Park. A fire truck barrels by, its sirens whining. *Scratch your head or you'll be dead.* I don't even remember where I learned that childhood rhyme or the dictum that demanded you scratch your head every time you heard a siren, lest the next siren be for you. But I do know when I started doing it, and now it's become second nature. Still, in a place like Manhattan, where the sirens are always blaring, it can become exhausting to keep up.

It's early evening now and the aggressive heat has mellowed, and it's like everyone senses that it's safe to go out because they're mobbing the place: spreading out picnics on the lawn, pushing jogging strollers up the paths, floating in canoes along the lily-padded lake.

Much as I like seeing all the people doing their thing, it all makes me feel exposed. I don't get how other people in the public eye do it. Sometimes I see pictures of Brad Pitt with his gaggle of kids in Central Park, just playing on swings, and clearly he was followed by paparazzi but he still looks like he's having a normal day with his family. Or maybe not. Pictures can be pretty deceptive.

Thinking about all this and passing happy people enjoying a summer evening, I start to feel like a moving target, even though I have my cap pulled low and my shades are on and I'm without Bryn. When Bryn and I are together, it's almost impossible to fly under the radar. I'm seized with this paranoia, not even so much that I'll get photographed or hounded by a mob of autograph seekers—though I really don't want to deal with that right now—but that I'll be mocked as the only person in the entire park who's alone, even though this obviously isn't the case. But still, I feel like any second people will start pointing, making fun of me.

So, this is how it's become? This is what *I've* become? A walking contradiction? I'm surrounded by people and feel alone. I claim to crave a bit of normalcy but now that I have some, it's like I don't know what to do with it, don't know how to be a normal person anymore.

I wander toward the Ramble, where the only people I'm likely to bump into are the kind who don't want to be found. I buy a couple of hot dogs and down them in a few bites, and it's only then that I realize I haven't eaten all day, which makes me think about lunch—and the Vanessa LeGrande debacle.

What happened back there? I mean, you've been known to get testy with reporters, but that was just an amateur-hour move, I tell myself.

I'm just tired, I justify. *Overtaxed.* I think of the tour and it's like the mossy ground next to me opens up and starts whirring.

Sixty-seven nights. I try to rationalize it. *Sixty-seven nights is nothing.* I try to divide up the number, to fractionalize it, to do something to make it smaller, but nothing divides evenly into sixty-seven. So I break it up. Fourteen countries, thirty-nine cities, a few hundred hours on a tour bus. But the math just makes the whirring go faster and I start to feel dizzy. I grab hold of the tree trunk and run my hand against the bark, which reminds me of Oregon and makes the earth at least close up for the time being.

I can't help but think about how, when I was younger, I'd read about the legions of artists who imploded—

Morrison, Joplin, Cobain, Hendrix. They disgusted me. *They got what they wanted and then what did they do? Drugged themselves to oblivion. Or shot their heads off. What a bunch of assholes.*

Well, take a look at yourself now. You're no junkie but you're not much better.

I would change if I could, but so far, ordering myself to shut up and enjoy the ride hasn't had much of an impact. If the people around me knew how I feel, they'd laugh at me. No, that's not true. Bryn wouldn't laugh. She'd be baffled by my inability to bask in what I've worked so hard to accomplish.

But have I worked so hard? There's this assumption among my family, Bryn, the rest of the band—well, at least there used to be among those guys—that I somehow deserve all this, that the acclaim and wealth is payback. I've never really bought that. Karma's not like a bank. Make a deposit, take a withdrawal. But more and more, I *am* starting to suspect that all this *is* payback for something—only not the good kind.

I reach for a cigarette, but my pack's empty. I stand up and dust off my jeans and make my way out of the park. The sun is starting to dip to the west, a bright blaring ball tilting toward the Hudson and leaving a collage of peach and purple streaks across the sky. It really is pretty and for a second I force myself to admire it.

I turn south on Seventh, stop at a deli, grab some smokes, and then head downtown. I'll go back to the hotel, get some room service, maybe fall asleep early for once. Outside Carnegie Hall, taxis are pulling up, dropping off people for tonight's performances. An old woman in pearls and heels teeters out of a taxi, her stooped-over companion in a tux holding onto her elbow. Watching them stumble off together, I feel something in my chest lurch. *Look at the sunset*, I tell myself. *Look at something with beauty.* But when I look back up at the sky, the streaks have darkened to the color of a bruise.

Prissy, temperamental asshole. That's what the reporter was calling me. She was a piece of work, but on that particular point, she was speaking the truth.

My gaze returns to earth and when it does, it's *her* eyes I see. Not the way I used to see them—around every corner, behind my own closed lids at the start of each day. Not in the way I used to imagine them in the eyes of every other girl I laid on top of. No, this time it really is her eyes. A photo of her, dressed in black, a cello leaning against one shoulder like a tired child. Her hair is up in one of those buns that seem to be a requisite for classical musicians. She used to wear it up like that for recitals and chamber music concerts, but with little pieces hanging down, to soften the severity of the look. There are no tendrils in this photo. I peer closer at the sign. YOUNG CONCERT SERIES PRESENTS MIA HALL.

A few months ago, Liz broke the unspoken embargo on all things Mia and mailed me a clip from the magazine *All About Us*. *I thought you should see this,* was scrawled on a sticky note. It was an article titled "Twenty Under 20," featuring upcoming "wunderkinds." There was a page on Mia, including a picture I could barely bring myself to glance at, and an article about her, that after a few rounds of deep breathing, I only managed to skim. The piece called her the "heir apparent to Yo-Yo Ma." In spite of myself, I'd smiled at that. Mia used to say that people who had no idea about the cello always described cellists as the next Yo-Yo Ma because he was their single point of reference. "What about Jacqueline Du Pré?" she'd always asked, referring to her own idol, a talented and tempestuous cellist who'd been stricken with multiple sclerosis at the age of twenty-eight and died about fifteen years later.

The *All About Us* article called Mia's playing "otherworldly" and then very graphically described the car accident that had killed her parents and little brother more than three years ago. That had surprised me. Mia hadn't been one to talk about that, to fish for sympathy points. But when I'd managed to make myself skim the piece again, I'd realized that it was a write-around, quotes taken from old newspaper accounts, but nothing directly from Mia herself.

I'd held onto the clipping for a few days, occasionally taking it out to glance over it. Having the thing in my wallet felt a little bit like carrying around a vial of plutonium. And for sure if Bryn caught me with an article about Mia there'd be explosions of the nuclear variety. So after a few more days, I threw it away and forced myself to forget it.

Now, I try to summon the details, to recall if it said anything about Mia leaving Juilliard or playing recitals at Carnegie Hall.

I look up again. Her eyes are still there, still staring at me. And I just know with as much certainty as I know anything in this world that she's playing tonight. I know even before I consult the date on the poster and see that the performance is for August thirteenth.

And before I know what I'm doing, before I can argue myself out of it, rationalize what a *terrible* idea this is, I'm walking toward the box office. *I don't want to see her,* I tell myself. *I won't see her. I only want to hear her.* The box office sign says that tonight is sold out. I could announce who I am or put in a call to my hotel's concierge or Aldous and probably get a ticket, but instead I leave it to fate. I present myself as an anonymous, if underdressed, young man and ask if there are any seats left.

"In fact, we're just releasing the rush tickets. I have a rear mezzanine, side. It's not the ideal view, but it's all that's left," the girl behind the glass window tells me.

"I'm not here for the view," I reply.

"I always think that, too," the girl says, laughing. "But people get particular about these kinds of things. That'll be twenty-five dollars."

I throw down my credit card and enter the cool, dim theater. I slide into my seat and close my eyes, remembering the last time I went to a cello concert somewhere this fancy. Five years ago, on our first date. Just as I did that night, I feel this mad rush of anticipation, even though I know that unlike that night, tonight I won't kiss her. Or touch her. Or even see her up close.

Tonight, I'll listen. And that'll be enough.

THREE

Mia woke up after four days, but we didn't tell her until the sixth day. It didn't matter because she seemed to already know. We sat around her hospital bed in the ICU, her taciturn grandfather having drawn the short straw, I guess, because he was the one chosen to break the news that her parents, Kat and Denny, had been killed instantly in the car crash that had landed her here. And that her little brother, Teddy, had died in the emergency room of the local hospital where he and Mia had been brought to before Mia was evacuated to Portland.

Nobody knew the cause of the crash. Did Mia have any memory of it?

Mia just lay there, blinking her eyes and holding onto my hand, digging her nails in so tightly it seemed like she'd never let me go. She shook her head and quietly said "no, no, no," over and over again, but without tears, and I wasn't sure if she was answering her grandfather's question or just negating the whole situation. *No!*

But then the social worker stepped in, taking over in her no-nonsense way. She told Mia about the operations she'd undergone so far, "triage, really, just to get you stable, and you're doing remarkably well," and then talked about the surgeries that she'd likely be facing in the coming months: First a surgery to reset the bone in her left leg with metal rods. Then another surgery a week or so after that, to harvest skin from the thigh of her uninjured leg. Then another to graft that skin onto the messed-up leg. Those two procedures, unfortunately, would leave some "nasty scars." But the injuries on her face, at least, could vanish completely with cosmetic surgery after a year. "Once you're through your nonelective surgeries, provided there aren't any complications—no infections from the splenectomy, no pneumonia, no problems with your lungs—we'll get you out of the hospital and into rehab," the social worker said. "Physical and occupational, speech and whatever else you need. We'll assess where you are in a few days." I was dizzy from this litany, but Mia seemed to hang on her every word, to pay more attention to the details of her surgeries than to the news of her family.

Later that afternoon, the social worker took the rest of us aside. We—Mia's grandparents and me—had been worried about Mia's reaction, or her lack of one. We'd expected screaming, hair pulling, something explosive, to match the horror of the news, to match our *own* grief. Her eerie quiet had all of us thinking the same thing: brain damage.

"No, that's not it," the social worker quickly reassured. "The brain is a fragile instrument and we may not know for a few weeks what specific regions have been affected, but young people are so very resilient and right now her neurologists are quite optimistic. Her motor control is generally good. Her language faculties don't seem too affected. She has weakness in her right side and her balance is off. If that's the extent of her brain injury, then she is fortunate."

We all cringed at that word. *Fortunate.* But the social worker looked at our faces. "*Very* fortunate because all of that is reversible. As for that reaction back there," she said, gesturing toward the ICU, "that is a typical response to such extreme psychological trauma. The brain can only handle so much, so it filters in a bit at a time,

digests slowly. She'll take it all in, but she'll need help."
Then she'd told us about the stages of grief, loaded us
up with pamphlets on post-traumatic stress disorder, and
recommended a grief counselor at the hospital for Mia
to see. "It might not be a bad idea for the rest of you,
too," she'd said.

We'd ignored her. Mia's grandparents weren't the
therapy types. And as for me, I had Mia's rehabilitation
to worry about, not my own.

The next round of surgeries started almost immediately, which I found cruel. Mia had just come back from
the brink of it, only to be told her family was dead, and
now she had to go under the knife again. Couldn't they
cut the girl a break? But the social worker had explained
that the sooner Mia's leg was fixed, the sooner Mia
would be mobile, and the sooner she could really start
to heal. So her femur was set with pins; skin grafts were
taken. And with speed that made me breathless, she was
discharged from the hospital and dispatched to a rehab
center, which looked like a condo complex, with flat
paths crisscrossing the grounds, which were just beginning to bloom with spring flowers when Mia arrived.

She'd been there less than a week, a determined,
teeth-gritted terrifying week, when the envelope came.

Juilliard. It had been so many things to me before.
A foregone conclusion. A point of pride. A rival. And

then I'd just forgotten about it. I think we all had. But life was churning outside Mia's rehab center, and somewhere out there in the world, that other Mia—the one who had two parents, a brother, and a fully working body—still continued to exist. And in that other world, some judges had listened to Mia play a few months earlier and had gone on processing her application, and it had gone through the various motions until a final judgment was made, and that final judgment was before us now. Mia's grandmother had been too nervous to open the envelope, so she waited for me and Mia's grandfather before she sliced into it with a mother-of-pearl letter opener.

Mia got in. Had there ever been any question?

We all thought the acceptance would be good for her, a bright spot on an otherwise bleak horizon.

"And I've already spoken to the dean of admissions and explained your situation, and they've said you can put off starting for a year, two if you need," Mia's grandmother had said as she'd presented Mia with the news and the generous scholarship that had accompanied the acceptance. Juilliard had actually suggested the deferral, wanting to make sure that Mia was able to play up to the school's rigorous standards, if she chose to attend.

"No," Mia had said from the center's depressing common room in that dead-flat voice she had spoken in since the accident. None of us was quite sure whether this was from emotional trauma or if this was Mia's affect now, her newly rearranged brain's way of speaking. In spite of the social worker's continued reassurances, in spite of her therapists' evaluations that she was making solid progress, we still worried. We discussed these things in hushed tones after we left her alone on the nights that I couldn't con myself into staying over.

"Well, don't be hasty," her grandmother had replied. "The world might look different in a year or two. You might still want to go."

Mia's grandmother had thought Mia was refusing Juilliard. But I knew better. I knew *Mia* better. It was the deferral she was refusing.

Her grandmother argued with Mia. September was five months away. Too soon. And she had a point. Mia's leg was still in one of those boot casts, and she was just starting to walk again. She couldn't open a jar because her right hand was so weak, and she would often blank on the names of simple things, like scissors. All of which the therapists said was to be expected and would likely pass—in good time. But five months? That wasn't long.

Mia asked for her cello that afternoon. Her grandmother had frowned, worried that this foolishness would waylay Mia's recovery. But I jumped out of my chair and ran to my car and was back with the cello by the time the sun set.

After that, the cello became her therapy: physical, emotional, mental. The doctors were amazed at Mia's upper-body strength—what her old music teacher Professor Christie had called her "cello body," broad shoulders, muscular arms—and how her playing brought that strength back, which made the weakness in her right arm go away and strengthened her injured leg. It helped with the dizziness. Mia closed her eyes as she played, and she claimed that this, along with grounding her two feet on the floor, helped her balance. Through playing, Mia revealed the lapses she tried to hide in everyday conversation. If she wanted a Coke but couldn't remember the word for it, she'd cover up and just ask for orange juice. But with cello, she would be honest about the fact that she remembered a Bach suite she'd been working on a few months ago but not a simple étude she'd learned as a child; although once Professor Christie, who came down once a week to work with her, showed it to her, she'd pick it right up. This gave the speech therapists and neurologists clues as to the hopscotch way her brain had been impacted, and they tailored their therapies accordingly.

But mostly, the cello improved her mood. It gave her

something to do every day. She stopped speaking in the monotone and started to talk like Mia again, at least when she was talking about music. Her therapists altered her rehabilitation plan, allowing her to spend more time practicing. "We don't really get how music heals the brain," one of her neurologists told me one afternoon as he listened to her play to a group of patients in the common room, "but we know that it does. Just look at Mia."

She left the rehab center after four weeks, two weeks ahead of schedule. She could walk with a cane, open a jar of peanut butter, and play the hell out of Beethoven.

⌒

That article, the "Twenty Under 20" thing from *All About Us* that Liz showed me, I do remember one thing about it. I remember the not-just-implied but overtly stated connection between Mia's "tragedy" and her "otherworldly" playing. And I remember how that pissed me off. Because there was something insulting in that. As if the only way to explain her talent was to credit some supernatural force. Like what'd they think, that her dead family was inhabiting her body and playing a celestial choir through her fingers?

But the thing was, there *was* something otherworldly that happened. And I know because I was there. I witnessed it: I saw how Mia went from being a very talented player to something altogether different. In the space of five months, something magical and grotesque transformed her. So, yes, it was all related to her "tragedy," but Mia was the one doing the heavy lifting. She always had been.

～

She left for Juilliard the day after Labor Day. I drove her to the airport. She kissed me good-bye. She told me that she loved me more than life itself. Then she stepped through security.

She never came back.

FOUR

The bow is so old, its horsehair is glue
Sent to the factory, just like me and like you
So how come they stayed your execution?
The audience roars its standing ovation

"DUST"

COLLATERAL DAMAGE, TRACK 9

When the lights come up after the concert, I feel drained, lugubrious, as though my blood has been secreted out of me and replaced with tar. After the applause dies down, the people around me stand up, they talk about the concert, about the beauty of the Bach, the mournfulness of the Elgar, the risk—that paid off—of throwing in the contemporary John Cage piece. But it's the Dvořák that's eating up all the oxygen in the room, and I can understand why.

When Mia used to play her cello, her concentration was always written all over her body: a crease folded across her forehead. Her lips, pursed so tightly they sometimes lost all their color, as if all her blood was requisitioned to her hands.

There was a little bit of that happening with the earlier pieces tonight. But when she got to the Dvořák, the final piece of her recital, something came over her. I don't know if she hit her groove or if this was her signature piece, but instead of hunching over her cello, her body seemed to expand, to bloom, and the music filled the open spaces around it like a flowering vine. Her strokes were broad and happy and bold, and the sound that filled the auditorium seemed to channel this pure emotion, like the very intention of the composer was spiraling through the room. And the look on her face, with her eyes upward, a small smile playing on her lips, I don't know how to describe it without sounding like one of these clichéd magazine articles, but she seemed so at one with the music. Or maybe just happy. I guess I always knew she was capable of this level of artistry, but witnessing it fucking blew me away. Me and everyone else in that auditorium, judging by the thunderous applause she got.

The houselights are up now, bright and bouncing off the blond wood chairs and the geometric wall panels, making the floor start to swim. I sink back down into the nearest chair and try not to think about the Dvořák—or the other things: the way she wiped her hand on her skirt in between pieces, the way she cocked her head in time to some invisible orchestra, all gestures that are way too familiar to me.

Grasping onto the chair in front of me for balance, I stand up again. I make sure my legs are working and the ground isn't spinning and then will one leg to follow the other toward the exit. I am shattered, exhausted. All I want to do now is go back to my hotel to down a couple of Ambien or Lunesta or Xanax or whatever's in my medicine cabinet—and end this day. I want to go to sleep and wake up and have this all be over.

"Excuse me, Mr. Wilde."

I normally have a thing about enclosed spaces, but if there is one place in the city where I'd expect the safety of anonymity, it's Carnegie Hall for a classical concert. All through the concert and intermission, no one gave me a second glance, except a pair of old biddies who I think were mostly just dismayed by my jeans. But this guy is about my age; he's an usher, the only person within fifty feet under the age of thirty-five, the only person around here likely to own a Shooting Star album.

I'm reaching into my pocket for a pen that I don't

have. The usher looks embarrassed, shaking his head and his hands simultaneously. "No, no, Mr. Wilde. I'm not asking for an autograph." He lowers his voice. "It's actually against the rules, could get me fired."

"Oh," I say, chastened, confused. For a second I wonder if I'm about to get dressed-down for dressing down.

The usher says: "Ms. Hall would like you to come backstage."

It's noisy with the after-show hubbub, so for a second I assume I've misheard him. I think he says that *she* wants me backstage. But that can't be right. He must be talking about *the* hall, not *Mia* Hall.

But before I can get him to clarify, he's leading me by the elbow back toward the staircase and down to the main lobby and through a small door beside the stage and through a maze of corridors, the walls lined with framed sheet music. And I'm allowing myself to be led; it's like the time when I was ten years old and was sent to the principal's office for throwing a water balloon in class, and all I could do was follow Mrs. Linden down the hallways and wonder what awaited me behind the main office doors. I have that same feeling. That I'm in trouble for something, that Aldous didn't really give me the evening off and I'm about to be reamed out for missing a photo shoot or pissing off a reporter or being the antisocial lone wolf in danger of breaking up the band.

And so I don't really process it, don't let myself hear it or believe it or think about it until the usher leads me to a small room and opens the door and closes it, and suddenly she's there. Really there. A flesh-and-blood person, not a specter.

My first impulse is not to grab her or kiss her or yell at her. I simply want to touch her cheek, still flushed from the night's performance. I want to cut through the space that separates us, measured in feet—not miles, not continents, not years—and to take a callused finger to her face. I want to touch her to make sure it's really her, not one of those dreams I had so often after she left when I'd see her as clear as day, be ready to kiss her or take her to me only to wake up with Mia just beyond reach.

But I can't touch her. This is a privilege that's been revoked. Against my will, but still. Speaking of will, I have to mentally hold my arm in place, to keep the trembling from turning it into a jackhammer.

The floor is spinning, the vortex is calling, and I'm itching for one of my pills, but there's no reaching for one now. I take some calming breaths to preempt a panic attack. I work my jaw in a vain attempt to get my mouth to say some words. I feel like I'm alone on a stage, no band, no equipment, no memory of any of our songs, being watched by a million people. I feel like an hour has gone by as I stand here in front of Mia Hall, speechless as a newborn.

The first time we ever met in high school, I spoke first. I asked Mia what cello piece she'd just played. A simple question that started everything.

This time, it's Mia who asks the question: "Is it really you?" And her voice, it's exactly the same. I don't know why I'd expect it to be different except that everything's different now.

Her voice jolts me back to reality. Back to the reality of the past three years. There are so many things that demand to be said. *Where did you go? Do you ever think about me? You've ruined me. Are you okay?* But of course, I can't say any of that.

I start to feel my heart pound and a ringing in my ears, and I'm about to lose it. But strangely, just when the panic starts to peak, some survival instinct kicks in, the one that allows me to step onto a stage in front of thousands of strangers. A calm steals over me as I retreat from myself, pushing me into the background and letting that other person take over. "In the flesh," I respond in kind. Like it's the most normal thing in the world for me to be at her concert and for her to have beckoned me into her sanctum. "Good concert," I add because it seems like the thing to say. It also happens to be true.

"Thank you," she says. Then she cringes. "I just, I can't believe you're *here*."

I think of the three-year restraining order she basically took out on me, which I violated tonight. *But you called me down*, I want to say. "Yeah. I guess they'll let any old riffraff in Carnegie Hall," I joke. In my nervousness, though, the quip comes out surly.

She smooths her hands on the fabric of her skirt. She's already changed out of her formal black gown into a long, flowy skirt and a sleeveless shirt. She shakes her head, tilts her face toward mine, all conspiratorial. "Not really. No punks allowed. Didn't you see the warning on the marquee? I'm surprised you didn't get arrested just for setting foot in the lobby."

I know she's trying to return my bad joke with one of her own and part of me is thankful for that, and thankful to see a glimmer of her old sense of humor. But another part, the churlish part, wants to remind her of all of the chamber music concerts, string quartets, and recitals I once sat through. Because of her. With her. "How'd you know I was here?" I ask.

"Are you kidding? Adam Wilde in Zankel Hall. At the intermission, the entire backstage crew was buzzing about it. Apparently, a lot of Shooting Star fans work at Carnegie Hall."

"I thought I was being incognito," I say. To her feet. The only way to survive this conversation is to have it with Mia's sandals. Her toenails are painted pale pink.

"You? Impossible," she replies. "So, how are you?"

How am I? Are you for real? I force my eyes upward and look at Mia for the first time. She's still beautiful. Not in an obvious Vanessa LeGrande or Bryn Shraeder kind of way. In a quiet way that's always been devastating to me. Her hair, long and dark, is down now, swimming damply against her bare shoulders, which are still milky white and covered with the constellation of freckles that I used to kiss. The scar on her left shoulder, the one that used to be an angry red welt, is silvery pink now. Almost like the latest rage in tattoo accessories. Almost pretty.

Mia's eyes reach out to meet mine, and for a second I fear that my facade will fall apart. I look away.

"Oh, you know? Good. Busy," I answer.

"Right. Of course. Busy. Are you on tour?"

"Yep. Off to London tomorrow."

"Oh. I'm off to Japan tomorrow."

Opposite directions, I think and am surprised when Mia actually says it out loud. "Opposite directions." The words just hang out there, ominous. Suddenly, I feel the vortex begin to churn again. It's going to swallow us both if I don't get away. "Well, I should probably go." I hear the calm person impersonating Adam Wilde say from what sounds like several feet away.

I think I see something darken her expression, but I can't really tell because every part of my body is undulating, and I swear I might just come inside-out right here. But as I'm losing it, that other Adam is still functioning. He's reaching out his hand toward Mia even though the thought of me giving Mia Hall a business handshake is maybe one of the saddest things I've ever imagined.

Mia looks down at my outstretched hand, opens her mouth to say something, and then just sighs. Her face hardens into a mask as she reaches out her own hand to take mine.

The tremor in my hand has become so normal, so nonstop, that it's generally imperceptible to me. But as soon as my fingers close around Mia's, the thing I notice is that it stops and suddenly it goes quiet, like when the squall of feedback is suddenly cut when someone switches off an amp. And I could linger here forever.

Except this is a handshake, nothing more. And in a few seconds my hand is at my side and it's like I've transferred a little of my crazy to Mia because it looks like her own hand is trembling. But I can't be sure be-cause I'm drifting away on a fast current.

And the next thing I know, I hear the door to her dressing room click behind me, leaving me out here on the rapids and Mia back there on the shore.

FIVE

I know it's really cheesy—crass even—to compare my being dumped to the accident that killed Mia's family, but I can't help it. Because for me, at any rate, the aftermath felt exactly the same. For the first few weeks, I'd wake up in a fog of disbelief. *That didn't really happen, did it? Oh, fuck, it did.* Then I'd be doubled over. Fist to the gut. It took a few weeks for it all to sink in. But unlike with the accident—when I had to be there, be present, help, be the person to lean on—after she left, I was all alone. There was nobody to step up to the plate for. So

I just let everything fall away and then everything just stopped.

I moved home, back to my parents' place. Just grabbed a pile of stuff from my room at the House of Rock and left. Left everything. School. The band. My life. A sudden and wordless departure. I balled up in my boy bed. I was worried that everyone would bang down the door and force me to explain myself. But that's the thing with death. The whisper of its descent travels fast and wide, and people must've known I'd become a corpse because nobody even came to view the body. Well, except relentless Liz, who stopped by once a week to drop off a CD mix of whatever new music she was loving, which she cheerfully stacked on top of the untouched CD she'd left the week before.

My parents seemed baffled by my return. But then, bafflement was pretty typical where I was concerned. My dad had been a logger, and then when that industry went belly-up he'd gotten a job on the line at an electronics plant. My mom worked for the university catering department. They were one another's second marriages, their first marital forays both disastrous and childless and never discussed; I only found out about them from an aunt and uncle when I was ten. They had me when they were older, and I'd apparently come as a surprise. And my mom liked to say that everything that I'd done—from my mere existence to becoming a musician, to falling in love with a girl like Mia, to going to college, to having the band become so popular, to dropping out of college, to dropping out of the band—was a surprise, too. They accepted my return home with no questions. Mom brought me little trays of food and coffee to my room, like I was a prisoner.

For three months, I lay in my childhood bed, wishing myself as comatose as Mia had been. That had to be easier than this. My sense of shame finally roused me. I was nineteen years old, a college dropout, living in my parents' house, unemployed, a layabout, a cliché. My parents had been cool about the whole thing, but the reek of my pathetic was starting to make me sick. Finally, right after the New Year, I asked my father if there were any jobs at the plant.

"You sure this is what you want?" he'd asked me. It wasn't what I wanted. But I couldn't have what I wanted. I'd just shrugged. I'd heard him and my mom arguing about it, her trying to get him to talk me out of it. "Don't you want more than that for him?" I heard her shout-whisper from downstairs. "Don't you want him back in school at the very least?"

"It's not about what I want," he'd answered.

So he asked around human resources, got me an interview, and a week later, I began work in the data-entry department. From six thirty in the morning to three thirty in the afternoon, I would sit in a windowless room, plugging in numbers that had no meaning to me.

On my first day of work, my mother got up early to make me a huge breakfast I couldn't eat and a pot of coffee that wasn't nearly strong enough. She stood over me in her ratty pink bathrobe, a worried expression on her face. When I got up to leave, she shook her head at me.

"What?" I asked.

"You working at the plant," she said, staring at me solemnly. "*This* doesn't surprise me. *This* is what I would've expected from a son of mine." I couldn't tell if the bitterness in her voice was meant for her or me.

The job sucked, but whatever. It was brainless. I came home and slept all afternoon and then woke up and read and dozed from ten o'clock at night until five in the morning, when it was time to get up for work. The schedule was out of sync with the living world, which was fine by me

A few weeks earlier, around Christmas, I'd still held a candle of hope. Christmas was when Mia had initially planned to come home. The ticket she'd bought for New York was a round-trip, and the return date was

December nineteenth. Though I knew it was foolish, I somehow thought she'd come see me, she'd offer some explanation—or, better yet, a massive apology. Or we'd find that this had all been some huge and horrible misunderstanding. She'd been emailing me daily but they hadn't gotten through, and she'd show up at my door, livid about my not having returned her emails, the way she used to get pissed off at me for silly things, like how nice I was, or was not, to her friends.

But December came and went, a monotony of gray, of muted Christmas carols coming from downstairs. I stayed in bed.

It wasn't until February that I got a visitor home from a back East college.

"Adam, Adam, you have a guest," my mom said, gently rapping at my door. It was around dinnertime and I was sacked out, the middle of the night to me. In my haze, I thought it was Mia. I bolted upright but saw from my mother's pained expression that she knew she was delivering disappointing news. "It's Kim!" she said with forced joviality.

Kim? I hadn't heard from Mia's best friend since August, not since she'd taken off for school in Boston. And all at once, it hit me that her silence was as much a betrayal as Mia's. Kim and I had never been buddies when Mia and I were together. At least not before the accident. But after, we'd been soldered somehow. I hadn't realized that Mia and Kim were a package deal, one with the other. Lose one, lose the other. But then, how else would it be?

But now, here was Kim. Had Mia sent her as some sort of an emissary? Kim was smiling awkwardly, hugging herself against the damp night. "Hey," she said. "You're hard to find."

"I'm where I've always been," I said, kicking off the covers. Kim, seeing my boxers, turned away until I'd pulled on a pair of jeans. I reached for a pack of cigarettes. I'd started smoking a few weeks before. Everyone at the plant seemed to. It was the only reason to take a break. Kim's eyes widened in surprise, like I'd just pulled out a Glock. I put the cigarettes back down without lighting up.

"I thought you'd be at the House of Rock, so I went there. I saw Liz and Sarah. They fed me dinner. It was nice to see them." She stopped and appraised my room. The rumpled, sour blankets, the closed shades. "Did I wake you?"

"I'm on a weird schedule."

"Yeah. Your mom told me. *Data entry?*" She didn't bother to try to mask her surprise.

I was in no mood for small talk or condescension. "So, what's up, Kim?"

She shrugged. "Nothing. I'm in town for break. We all went to Jersey to see my grandparents for Hanukkah, so this is the first time I've been back and I wanted to stop and say hi."

Kim looked nervous. But she also looked concerned. It was an expression I recognized well. The one that said *I* was the patient now. In the distant night I heard a siren. Reflexively, I scratched my head.

"Do you still see her?" I asked.

"What?" Kim's voice chirped in surprise.

I stared at her. And slowly repeated the question. "Do you still see Mia?"

"Y—Yes," Kim stumbled. "I mean, not a lot. We're both busy with school, and New York and Boston are four hours apart. But yes. Of course."

Of course. It was the certainty that did it. That made something murderous rise up in me. I was glad there was nothing heavy within reaching distance.

"Does she know you're here?"

"No. I came as your friend."

"As *my* friend?"

Kim blanched from the sarcasm in my voice, but that girl was always tougher than she seemed. She didn't back down or leave. *"Yes,"* she whispered.

"Tell me, then, *friend*. Did Mia, *your* friend, your BFF, did she tell you why she dumped me? Without a word? Did she happen to mention that to you at all? Or didn't I come up?"

"Adam, please . . ." Kim's voice was an entreaty.

"No, please, Kim. Please, because I haven't got a clue."

Kim took a deep breath and then straightened her posture. I could practically see the resolve stiffening up her spine, vertebra by vertebra, the lines of loyalty being drawn. "I didn't come here to talk about Mia. I came here to see you, and I don't think I should discuss Mia with you or vice versa."

She'd adopted the tone of a social worker, an impartial third party, and I wanted to smack her for it. For all of it. Instead, I just exploded. "Then what the fuck are you doing here? What good are you then? Who are you to me? Without her, who are you? You're nothing! A nobody!"

Kim stumbled back, but when she looked up, instead of looking angry, she looked at me full of tenderness. It made me want to throttle her even more. "Adam—" she began.

"Get the hell out of here," I growled. "I don't want to see you again!"

The thing with Kim was, you didn't have to tell her twice. She left without another word.

That night, instead of sleeping, instead of reading, I paced my room for four hours. As I walked back and forth, pushing permanent indentations into the tread of my parents' cheap shag carpeting, I felt something febrile growing inside of me. It felt alive and inevitable, the way a puke with a nasty hangover sometimes is. I felt it itching its way through my body, begging for release, until it finally came tearing out of me with such force that first I punched my wall, and then, when that didn't hurt enough, my window. The shards of glass sliced into my knuckles with a satisfying ache followed by the cold blast of a February night. The shock seemed to wake something slumbering deep within me.

Because that was the night I picked up my guitar for the first time in a year.

And that was the night I started writing songs again.

Within two weeks, I'd written more than ten new songs. Within a month, Shooting Star was back together and playing them. Within two months, we'd signed with a major label. Within four months, we were recording *Collateral Damage*, comprised of fifteen of the songs I'd written from the chasm of my childhood bedroom. Within a year, *Collateral Damage* was on the

Billboard charts and Shooting Star was on the cover of national magazines.

It's occurred to me since that I owe Kim either an apology or a thank-you. Maybe both. But by the time I came to this realization, it seemed like things were too far gone to do anything about it. And, the truth is, I still don't know what I'd say to her.

SIX

I'll be your mess, you be mine
That was the deal that we had signed
I bought a hazmat suit to clean up your waste
Gas masks, gloves, to keep us safe
But now I'm alone in an empty room
Staring down immaculate doom

"MESSY"

COLLATERAL DAMAGE, TRACK 2

When I get onto the street, my hands are quaking and my insides feel like they're staging a coup. I reach for my pills, but the bottle is empty. *Fuck!* Aldous must've fed me the last one in the cab. Do I have more at the hotel? I've got to get some before tomorrow's flight. I grab for my phone and remember that I left it back at the hotel in some boneheaded attempt to disconnect.

People are swarming around and their gazes are lingering a little too long on me. I can't deal with being recognized right now. I can't deal with anything. I don't want this. I don't want *any* of this.

I just want out. Out of my existence. I find myself wishing that a lot lately. Not be dead. Or kill myself. Or any of that kind of stupid shit. It's more that I can't help thinking that if I'd never been born in the first place, I wouldn't be facing those sixty-seven nights, I wouldn't be right here, right now, having just endured that conversation with her. *It's your own fault for coming tonight*, I tell myself. *You should've left well enough alone.*

I light a cigarette and hope that will steady me enough to walk back to the hotel where I'll call Aldous and get everything straightened out and maybe even sleep a few hours and get this disastrous day behind me once and for all.

"You should quit."

Her voice jars me. But it also somehow calms me. I look up. There's Mia, face flushed, but also, oddly, smiling. She's breathing hard, like she's been running. Maybe she gets chased by fans, too. I imagine that old couple in the tux and pearls tottering after her.

I don't even have time to feel embarrassed because *Mia is here again*, standing in front of me like when we still shared the same space and time and bumping into each other, though always a happy coincidence, was nothing unusual, not the slightest bit extraordinary. For a second I think of that line in *Casablanca* when Bogart says: Of all the gin joints in the world, she has to walk into mine. But then I remind myself that I walked into *her* gin joint.

Mia covers the final few feet between us slowly, like I'm a cagey cat that needs to be brought in. She eyes the cigarette in my hand. "Since when do you smoke?" she asks. And it's like the years between us are gone, and Mia has forgotten that she no longer has the right to get on my case.

Even if in this instance it's deserved. Once upon a time, I'd been adamantly straightedge where nicotine was concerned. "I know. It's a cliché," I admit.

She eyes me, the cigarette. "Can I have one?"

"You?" When Mia was like six or something, she'd read some kid's book about a girl who got her dad to quit smoking and then she'd decided to lobby her mom, an on-again-off-again-smoker, to quit. It had taken Mia months to prevail upon Kat, but prevail she did. By the time I met them, Kat didn't smoke at all. Mia's dad, Denny, puffed on a pipe, but that seemed mostly for show. "*You* smoke now?" I ask her.

"No," Mia replies. "But I just had a really intense experience and I'm told cigarettes calm your nerves."

The intensity of a concert—it sometimes left me pent up and edgy. "I feel that way after shows sometimes," I say, nodding.

I shake out a cigarette for her; her hand is still trembling, so I keep missing the tip of the cigarette with my lighter. For a second I imagine grabbing her wrist to hold her steady. But I don't. I just chase the cigarette until the flame flashes across her eyes and lights the tip. She inhales and exhales, coughs a little. "I'm not talking about the concert, Adam," she says before taking another labored drag. "I'm talking about *you*."

Little pinpricks fire-cracker up and down my body. *Just calm down*, I tell myself. *You just make her nervous, showing up all out of the blue like that.* Still, I'm flattered that I matter—even if it's just enough to scare her.

We smoke in silence for a while. And then I hear something gurgle. Mia shakes her head in dismay and looks down at her stomach. "Remember how I used to get before concerts?"

Back in the day, Mia would get too nervous to eat before shows, so afterward she was usually ravenous. Back then, we'd go eat Mexican food at our favorite joint or hit a diner out on the highway for French fries with gravy and pie—Mia's dream meal. "How long since your last meal ?" I ask.

Mia peers at me again and stubs out her half-smoked cigarette. She shakes her head. "Zankel Hall? I haven't eaten for days. My stomach was rumbling all through the performance. I was sure even people in the balcony seats could hear it."

"Nope. Just the cello."

"That's a relief. I think."

We stand there in silence for a second. Her stomach gurgles again. "Fries and pie still the optimal meal?" I ask. I picture her in a booth back in our place in Oregon, waving her fork around, as she critiqued her own performance.

"Not pie. Not in New York. The diner pies are such disappointments. The fruit's almost always canned. And marionberry does not exist here. How is it possible that a fruit simply ceases to exist from one coast to another?"

How is it possible that a boyfriend ceases to exist from one day to another? "Couldn't tell you."

"But the French fries are good." She gives me a hopeful half smile.

"I like French fries," I say. *I like French fries?* I sound like a slow child in a made-for-TV movie.

Her eyes flutter up to meet mine. "Are you hungry?" she asks.

Am I ever.

⁓

I follow her across Fifty-seventh Street and then down Ninth Avenue. She walks quickly—without even a faint hint of the limp she had when she left—and purposefully, like New Yorkers do, pointing out landmarks here and there like a professional tour guide. It occurs to me I don't even know if she still lives here or if tonight was just a tour date.

You could just ask her, I tell myself. *It's a normal enough question.*

Yeah, but it's so normal that it's weird that I have to ask.

Well you've got to say something to her.

But just as I'm getting up the nerve, Beethoven's Ninth starts chiming from her bag. Mia stops her NYC monologue, reaches in for her cell phone, looks at the screen, and winces.

"Bad news?"

She shakes her head and gives a look so pained it has to be practiced. "No. But I have to take this."

She flips open the phone. "Hello. I know. Please calm down. I know. Look, can you just hold on one second?" She turns to me, her voice all smooth and professional now. "I know this is unbearably rude, but can you just give me five minutes?"

I get it. She just played a big show. She's got people calling. But even so, and in spite of the mask of apology she's wearing, I feel like a groupie being asked to wait in the back of the bus until the rock star's ready. But like the groupies always do, I acquiesce. The rock star is Mia. What else am I gonna do?

"Thank you," she says.

I let Mia walk a few paces ahead of me, to give her some privacy, but I still catch snippets of her end of the conversation. *I know it was important to you. To us. I promise I'll make it up to everyone.* She doesn't mention *me* once. In fact she seems to have forgotten about me back here entirely.

Which would be okay except that she's also oblivious to the commotion that my presence is creating along Ninth Avenue, which is full of bars and people loitering and smoking in front of them. People who double take as they recognize me, and yank out their cell phones and digital cameras to snap pictures.

I vaguely wonder if any of the shots will make it onto Gabber or one of the tabloids. It would be a dream for Vanessa LeGrande. And a nightmare with Bryn. Bryn is jealous enough of Mia as it is, even though she's never met her; she only knows about her. Even though she knows I haven't seen Mia in years, Bryn still complains: "It's hard competing with a ghost." As if Bryn Shraeder has to compete with anyone.

"Adam? Adam Wilde?" It's a real paparazzo with a telephoto lens about a half block away. "Yo, Adam. Can we get a shot? Just one shot," he calls.

Sometimes that works. Give them one minute of your face and they leave. But more often than not, it's like killing one bee and inviting the swarm's wrath.

"Yo, Adam. Where's Bryn?"

I put on my glasses, speed up, though it's too late for that. I stop walking and step out on to Ninth Avenue, which is clogged with taxis. Mia just keeps walking down the block, yapping away into her cell phone. The old Mia hated cell phones, hated people who talked on them in public, who dismissed one person's company to take a phone call from someone else. The old Mia would never have uttered the phrase *unbearably rude*.

I wonder if I should let her keep going. The thought of just jumping into a cab and being back at my hotel by the time she figures out I'm not behind her anymore gives me a certain gritty satisfaction. Let her do the wondering for a change.

But the cabs are all occupied, and, as if the scent of my distress has suddenly reached her, Mia swivels back around to see me, to see the photographer approaching me, brandishing his cameras like machetes. She looks back on to Ninth Avenue at the sea of cars. *Just go on, go on ahead*, I silently tell her. *Get your picture taken with me and your life becomes fodder for the mill. Just keep moving.*

But Mia's striding toward me, grabbing me by the wrist and, even though she's a foot shorter and sixty pounds lighter than me, I suddenly feel safe, safer in her custody than I do in any bouncer's. She walks right into the crowded avenue, stopping traffic just by holding up her other hand. A path opens for us, like we're the Israelites crossing the Red Sea. As soon as we're on the opposite curb, that opening disappears as the cabs all roar toward a green light, leaving my paparazzo stalker on the other side of the street. "It's near impossible to get a cab now," Mia tells me. "All the Broadway shows just let out."

"I've got about two minutes on that guy. Even if I get into a cab, he's gonna follow on foot in this traffic."

"Don't worry. He can't follow where we're going."

She jogs through the crowds, down the avenue, simultaneously pushing me ahead of her and shielding me like a defensive linebacker. She turns off on to a dark street full of tenement buildings. About halfway down the block, the cityscape of brick apartments abruptly gives way to a low area full of trees that's surrounded by a tall iron fence with a heavy-duty lock for which Mia magically produces the key. With a clank, the lock pops open. "In you go," she tells me, pointing to a hedge and a gazebo behind it. "Duck in the gazebo. I'll lock up."

I do as she says and a minute later she's back at my side. It's dark in here, the only light the soft glow of a nearby street lamp. Mia puts a finger to her lips and motions for me to crouch down.

"Where the hell did he go?" I hear someone call from the street.

"He went this way," says a woman, her voice thick with a New York accent. "I swear to ya."

"Well then, where is he?"

"What about that park?" the woman asks.

The clatter of the gate echoes through the garden. "It's locked," he says. In the darkness, I see Mia grin.

"Maybe he jumped over."

"It's like ten feet high," the guy replies. "You don't just leap over something like that."

"D'ya think he has superhuman strength?" the woman replies. "Ya could go inside and check for him."

"And rip my new Armani pants on the fence? A man has his limits. And it looks empty in there. He probably caught a cab. Which we should do. I got sources texting that Timberlake's at the Breslin."

I hear the sound of footsteps retreating and stay quiet for a while longer just to be safe. Mia breaks the silence.

"D'ya think he has superhuman strength?" she asks in a pitch-perfect imitation. Then she starts to laugh.

"I'm not gonna rip my new Armani pants," I reply. "A man has his limits."

Mia laughs even harder. The tension in my gut eases. I almost smile.

After her laughter dies down, she stands up, wipes the dirt from her backside, and sits down on the bench in the gazebo. I do the same. "That must happen to you all the time."

I shrug. "It's worse in New York and L.A. And London. But it's everywhere now. Even fans sell their pics to the tabloids."

"Everyone's in on the game, huh?" she says. Now this sounds more like the Mia I once knew, not like a Classical Cellist with a lofty vocabulary and one of those pan-Euro accents like Madonna's.

"Everyone wants their cut," I say. "You get used to it."

"You get used to a lot of things," Mia acknowledges.

I nod in the darkness. My eyes have adjusted so I can see that the garden is pretty big, an expanse of grass bisected by brick paths and ringed by flower beds. Every now and then, a tiny light flashes in the air. "Are those fireflies?" I ask.

"Yes."

"In the middle of the city?"

"Right. It used to amaze me, too. But if there's a patch of green, those little guys will find it and light it up. They only come for a few weeks a year. I always wonder where they go the rest of the time."

I ponder that. "Maybe they're still here, but just don't have anything to light up about."

"Could be. The insect version of seasonal affective disorder, though the buggers should try living in Oregon if they really want to know what a depressing winter is like."

"How'd you get the key to this place?" I ask. "Do you have to live around here?"

Mia shakes her head, then nods. "Yes, you do have to live in the area to get a key, but I don't. The key belongs to Ernesto Castorel. Or did belong to. When he was a guest conductor at the Philharmonic, he lived nearby and the garden key came with his sublet. I was having roommate issues at the time, which is a repeating theme in my life, so I wound up crashing at his place a lot, and after he left, I 'accidentally' took the key."

I don't know why I should feel so sucker-punched. *You've been with so many girls since Mia you've lost count*, I reason with myself. *It's not like you've been languishing in celibacy. You think she has?*

"Have you ever seen him conduct?" she asks me. "He always reminded me of you."

Except for tonight, I haven't so much as listened to classical music since you left. "I have no idea who you're talking about."

"Castorel? Oh, he's incredible. He came from the slums of Venezuela, and through this program that helps street kids by teaching them to play musical instruments, he wound up becoming a conductor at sixteen. He was the conductor of the Prague Philharmonic at twenty-four, and now he's the artistic director for the Chicago Symphony Orchestra and runs that very same program in Venezuela that gave him his start. He sort of breathes music. Same as you."

Who says I breathe music? Who says I even breathe? "Wow," I say, trying to push back against the jealousy I have no right to.

Mia looks up, suddenly embarrassed. "Sorry. I forget sometimes that the entire world isn't up on the minutiae of classical music. He's pretty famous in our world."

Yeah, well my *girlfriend is* really *famous in the rest of the world*, I think. But does she even know about Bryn and me? You'd have to have your head buried beneath a mountain not to have heard about us. Or you'd have to intentionally be avoiding any news of me. Or maybe you'd just have to be a classical cellist who doesn't read tabloids. "He sounds *swell*," I say.

Even Mia doesn't miss the sarcasm. "Not famous, like you, I mean," she says, her gushiness petering into awkwardness.

I don't answer. For a few seconds there's no sound, save for the river of traffic on the street. And then Mia's stomach gurgles again, reminding us that we've been waylaid in this garden. That we're actually on our way someplace else.

SEVEN

In a weird twisted way, Bryn and I met because of Mia. Well, one degree of separation, I guess. It was really because of the singer-songwriter Brooke Vega. Shooting Star had been slated to open for Brooke's former band, Bikini, the day of Mia's accident. When I hadn't been allowed to visit Mia in the ICU, Brooke had come to the hospital to try to create a diversion. She hadn't been successful. And that had been the last I'd seen of Brooke until the crazy time after *Collateral Damage* went double platinum.

Shooting Star was in L.A. for the MTV Movie

Awards. One of our previously recorded but never released songs had been put on the sound track for the movie *Hello, Killer* and was nominated for Best Song. We didn't win.

It didn't matter. The MTV Awards were just the latest in a string of ceremonies, and it had been a bumper crop in terms of awards. Just a few months earlier we'd picked up our Grammys for Best New Artist and Song of the Year for "Animate."

It was weird. You'd think that a platinum record, a pair of Grammys, a couple of VMAs would make your world, but the more it all piled on, the more the scene was making my skin crawl. There were the girls, the drugs, the ass-kissing, plus the hype—the constant hype. People I didn't know—and not groupies, but industry people—rushing up to me like they were my longtime friends, kissing me on both cheeks, calling me "babe," slipping business cards into my hand, whispering about movie roles or ads for Japanese beer, one-day shoots that would pay a million bucks.

I couldn't handle it, which was why once we'd finished doing our bit for the Movie Awards, I'd ducked out of the Gibson Amphitheater to the smokers' area. I was planning my escape when I saw Brooke Vega striding toward me. Behind her was a pretty, vaguely familiar-looking girl with long black hair and green eyes the size of dinner plates.

"Adam Wilde as I live and breathe," Brooke said, embracing me in a dervish hug. Brooke had recently gone solo and her debut album, *Kiss This*, had been racking up awards, too, so we'd been bumping into each other a lot at the various ceremonies. "Adam, this is Bryn Shraeder, but you probably know her as the fox nominated for The Best Kiss Award. Did you catch her fabulous smooch in *The Way Girls Fall?*"

I shook my head. "Sorry."

"I lost to a vampire-werewolf kiss. Girl-on-girl action doesn't have quite the same impact it used to," Bryn deadpanned.

"You were robbed!" Brooke interjected. "Both of you. It's a cryin' shame. But I'll leave you to lick your wounds or just get acquainted. I've got to get back and present. Adam, see you around, I hope. You should come to L.A. more often. You could use some color." She sauntered off, winking at Bryn.

We stood there in silence for a second. I offered a cigarette to Bryn. She shook her head, then looked at me with those eyes of hers, so unnervingly green. "That was a setup, in case you were wondering."

"Yeah, I was, sort of."

She shrugged, not in the least embarrassed. "I told Brooke I thought you were intriguing, so she took matters into her own hands. She and I, we're alike that way."

"I see."

"Does that bother you?"

"Why would it?"

"It would bother a lot of guys out here. Actors tend to be really insecure. Or gay."

"I'm not from here."

She smiled at that. Then she looked at my jacket. "You going AWOL or something?"

"You think they'll send the dogs on me?"

"Maybe, but it's L.A., so they'll be teeny-tiny Chihuahuas all trussed up in designer bags, so how much damage can they do. You want company?"

"Really? You don't have to stay and mourn your best-kiss loss?"

She looked me squarely in the eye, like she got the joke I was making and was in on it, too. Which I appreciated. "I prefer to celebrate or commiserate my kissing in private."

The only plan I had was to return to my hotel in the limo we had waiting. So instead I went with Bryn. She gave her driver the night off and grabbed the keys to her hulking SUV and drove us down the hill from Universal City toward the coast.

We cruised along the Pacific Coast Highway to a beach north of the city called Point Dume. We stopped on the way for a bottle of wine and some takeout sushi. By the time we reached the beach, a fog had descended over the inky water.

"June gloom," Bryn said, shivering in her short little green-and-black off-the-shoulder dress. "Never fails to freeze me."

"Don't you have a sweater or something?" I asked.

"It didn't complete the look."

"Here." I handed her my jacket.

She raised her eyebrows in surprise. "A gentleman."

We sat on the beach, sharing the wine straight out of the bottle. She told me about the film she'd recently wrapped and the one she was leaving to start shooting the following month. And she was trying to decide between one of two scripts to produce for the company she was starting.

"So you're a fundamentally lazy person?" I asked.

She laughed. "I grew up in this armpit town in Arizona, where all my life my mom told me how pretty I was, how I should be a model, an actress. She never even let me play outside in the sun—in Arizona!—because she didn't want me to mess up my skin. It was like all I had going for me was a pretty face." She turned to stare at me, and I could see the intelligence in her eyes, which were set, admittedly, in a very pretty face. "But fine, whatever, my face was the ticket out of there. But now Hollywood's the same way. Everyone has me pegged as an ingenue, another pretty face. But I know better. So if I want to prove I have a brain, if I want to play in the sunshine, so to speak, it's up to me to find the project that breaks me out. I feel like I'll be better positioned to do that if I'm a producer, too. It's all about control, really. I want to control everything, I guess."

"Yeah, but some things you can't control, no matter how hard you try."

Bryn stared out at the dark horizon, dug her bare toes into the cool sand. "I know," she said quietly. She turned to me. "I'm really sorry about your girlfriend. Mia, right?"

I coughed on the wine. That wasn't a name I was expecting to hear right now.

"I'm sorry. It's just when I asked Brooke about you, she told me how you two met. She wasn't gossiping or anything. But she was there, at the hospital, so she knew."

My heart thundered in my chest. I just nodded.

"My dad left when I was seven. It was the worst thing that ever happened to me," Bryn continued. "So I can't imagine losing someone like that."

I nodded again, swigged at the wine. "I'm sorry," I managed to say.

She nodded slightly in acknowledgment. "But at least they all died together. I mean that's got to be a blessing in a way. I know I wouldn't have wanted to wake up if the rest of my family had died."

The wine came sputtering out of my mouth, through my nose. It took me a few moments to regain my breath and my power of speech. When I did, I told Bryn that Mia wasn't dead. She'd survived the crash, had made a full recovery.

Bryn looked genuinely horrified, so much so that I felt sorry for her instead of for myself. "Lord, Adam. I'm so mortified. I just sort of assumed. Brooke said she'd never heard boo about Mia again and I would've come to the same conclusion. Shooting Star kind of disappears and then *Collateral Damage*, I mean, the lyrics are just so full of pain and anger and betrayal at being left behind. . . ."

"Yep," I said.

Then Bryn looked at me, the green of her eyes reflecting in the moonlight. And I could tell that she understood it all, without my having to say a word. Not having to explain, that felt like the biggest relief. "Oh, Adam. That's even worse in a way, isn't it?"

When Bryn said that, uttered out loud the thing that

to my never-ending shame I sometimes felt, I'd fallen in love with her a little bit. And I'd thought that was enough. That this implicit understanding and those first stirrings would bloom until my feelings for Bryn were as consuming as my love for Mia had once been.

I went back to Bryn's house that night. And all that spring I visited her on set up in Vancouver, then in Chicago, then in Budapest. Anything to get out of Oregon, away from the awkwardness that had formed like a thick pane of aquarium glass between me and the rest of the band. When she returned to L.A. that summer, she suggested I move into her Hollywood Hills house. "There's a guesthouse out back that I never use that we could turn into your studio."

The idea of getting out of Oregon, away from the rest of the band, from all that history, a fresh start, a house full of windows and light, a future with Bryn—it had felt so right at the time.

So that's how I became one half of a celebrity couple. Now I get my picture snapped with Bryn as we do stuff as mundane as grab a coffee from Starbucks or take a walk through Runyon Canyon.

I should be happy. I should be grateful. But the problem is, I never can get away from feeling that my fame isn't about me; it's about them. *Collateral Damage* was written with Mia's blood on my hands, and that was the record that launched me. And when I became really famous, it was for being with Bryn, so it had less to do with the music I was making than the girl I was with.

And the girl. She's great. Any guy would kill to be with her, would be proud to knock her up.

Except even at the start, when we were in that can't-get-enough-of-you phase, there was like some invisible wall between us. At first I tried to take it down, but it took so much effort to even make cracks. And then I got tired of trying. Then I justified it. *This was just how adult relationships were, how love felt once you had a few battle scars.*

Maybe that's why I can't let myself enjoy what we have. Why, in the middle of the night when I can't sleep, I go outside to listen to the lapping of the pool filter and obsess about the shit about Bryn that drives me crazy. Even as I'm doing it, I'm aware that it's minor league—the way she sleeps with a BlackBerry next to her pillow, the way she works out hours a day and catalogs every little thing she eats, the way she refuses to deviate from a plan or a schedule. And I know that there's plenty of great stuff to balance out the bad. She's generous as an oil baron and loyal as a pit bull.

I know I'm not easy to live with. Bryn tells me I'm withdrawn, evasive, cold. She accuses me—depending on her mood—of being jealous of her career, of being with her by accident, of cheating on her. It's not true. I haven't touched a groupie since we've been together; I haven't wanted to.

I always tell her that part of the problem is that we're hardly ever in the same place. If I'm not recording or touring, then Bryn's on location or off on one of her endless press junkets. What I don't tell her is that I can't imagine us being together more of the time. Because it's not like when we're in the same room everything's so great.

Sometimes, after Bryn's had a couple of glasses of wine, she'll claim that Mia's what's between us. "Why don't you just go back to your ghost?" she'll say. "I'm tired of competing with her."

"Nobody can compete with you," I tell her, kissing her on the forehead. And I'm not lying. Nobody *can* compete with Bryn. And then I tell her it's not Mia; it's not any girl. Bryn and I live in a bubble, a spotlight, a pressure cooker. It would be hard on any couple.

But I think we both know I'm lying. And the truth is, there isn't any avoiding Mia's ghost. Bryn and I wouldn't even be together if it weren't for her. In that twisted, incestuous way of fate, Mia's a part of our history, and we're among the shards of her legacy.

EIGHT

The clothes are packed off to Goodwill
I said my good-byes up on that hill
The house is empty, the furniture sold
Soon your smells will decay to mold
Don't know why I bother calling, ain't nobody answering
Don't know why I bother singing, ain't nobody listening

"DISCONNECT"
<u>COLLATERAL DAMAGE</u>, TRACK 10

Ever hear the one about that dog that spent its life chasing cars and finally caught one—and had no idea what to do with it?

I'm that dog.

Because here I am, alone with Mia Hall, something I've fantasized about now for more than three years, and it's like, now what?

We're at the diner that was apparently her destination, some random place way over on the west side of town. "It has a parking lot," Mia tells me when we arrive.

"Uh-huh," is all I can think to answer.

"I'd never seen a Manhattan restaurant with a parking lot before, which is why I first stopped in. Then I noticed that all the cabbies ate here and cabbies are usually excellent judges of good food, but then I wasn't sure because there *is* a parking lot, and free parking is a hotter commodity than good, cheap food."

Mia's babbling now. And I'm thinking: *Are we really talking about parking? When neither of us, as far as I can tell, owns a car here.* I'm hit again by how I don't know anything about her anymore, not the smallest detail.

The host takes us to a booth and Mia suddenly grimaces. "I shouldn't have brought you here. You probably never eat in places like this anymore."

She's right, actually, not because I prefer darkened, overpriced, exclusive eateries but because those are the ones I get taken to and those are the ones I generally get left alone in. But this place is full of old grizzled New Yorkers and cabbies, no one who'd recognize me. "No, this place is good," I say.

We sit down in a booth by the window, next to the vaunted parking lot. Two seconds later, a short, squat hairy guy is upon us. "Maestro," he calls to Mia. "Long time no see."

"Hi, Stavros."

Stavros plops down our menus and turns to me. He

raises a bushy eyebrow. "So, you finally bring your boy-friend for us to meet!"

Mia goes scarlet and, even though there's something insulting in her being so embarrassed by being tagged as my girlfriend, there's something comforting in see-ing her blush. This uncomfortable girl is more like the person I knew, the kind who would never have hushed conversations on cell phones.

"He's an old friend," Mia says.

Old friend? Is that a demotion or a promotion?

"Old friend, huh? You never come in here with any-one before. Pretty, talented girl like you. Euphemia!" he bellows. "Come out here. The maestro has a fellow!"

Mia's face has practically turned purple. When she looks up, she mouths: "The wife."

Out of the kitchen trundles the female equivalent of Stavros, a short, square-shaped woman with a face full of makeup, half of which seems to have melted onto her jowly neck. She wipes her hands on her greasy white apron and smiles at Mia, showing off a gold tooth. "I knew it!" she exclaims. "I knew you had a boyfriend you were hiding. Pretty girl like you. Now I see why you don't want to date my Georgie."

Mia purses her lips and raises her eyebrow at me; she gives Euphemia a faux-guilty smile. *Caught me.*

"Now, come on, leave them be," Stavros interjects, swatting Euphemia on the hip and edging in front of her. "Maestro, you want your usual?"

Mia nods.

"And your boyfriend?"

Mia actually cringes, and the silence at the table lengthens like dead air you still sometimes hear on college radio stations. "I'll have a burger, fries, and a beer," I say finally.

"Marvelous," Stavros says, clapping his hands together like I've just given him the cure for cancer. "Cheeseburger Deluxe. Side of onion rings. Your young man is too skinny. Just like you."

"You'll never have healthy kids if you don't put some meat on your bones," Euphemia adds.

Mia cradles her head in her hands, as though she's literally trying to disappear into her own body. After they leave, she peeks up. "God, that was, just, awkward. Clearly, they didn't recognize you."

"But they knew who *you* were. Wouldn't have pegged them as classical music buffs." Then I look down at my jeans, my black T-shirt, my beat-up sneaks. Once upon a time I'd been a classical music fan, too, so there's no telling.

Mia laughs. "Oh, they're not. Euphemia knows me from playing in the subway."

"You busked in the subway? Times that tough?" And then I realize what I just said and want to hit rewind. You don't ask someone like Mia if times are tough, even though I knew, financially, they weren't. Denny had taken out a supplemental life insurance policy in addition to the one he had through the teachers' union and that had left Mia pretty comfortable, although no one knew about the second policy right away. It was one of the reasons that, after the accident, a bunch of the musicians in town had played a series of benefit concerts and raised close to five thousand dollars for Mia's Juilliard fund. The outpouring had moved her grandparents—and me, too—but it had infuriated Mia. She'd refused to take the donation, calling it blood money, and when her grandfather had suggested that accepting other people's generosity was itself an act of generosity that might help people in the community feel better, she'd scoffed that it wasn't her job to make other people feel better.

But Mia just smiles. "It was a blast. And surprisingly lucrative. Euphemia saw me and when I came here to eat, she remembered me from the Columbus Circle station. She proudly informed me that she'd put a whole dollar into my case."

Mia's phone rings. We both stop to listen to the tinny melody. Beethoven plays on and on.

"Are you going to get that?" I ask.

She shakes her head, looking vaguely guilty.

No sooner does the ringing stop then it pipes up again.

"You're popular tonight."

"Not so much popular as in trouble. I was supposed to be at this dinner after the concert. Lots of bigwigs. Agents. Donors. I'm pretty sure that's either a Juilliard professor, someone from Young Concert Artists, or my management calling to yell at me."

"Or Ernesto?" I say as lightly as humanly possible. Because Stavros and Euphemia may have been on to something about Mia having some fancy-pants boy-friend—one that she doesn't drag into Greek diners. He just isn't me.

Mia looks uncomfortable again. "Could be."

"If you have people to talk to, or, you know, business to attend to, don't let me stand in your way."

"No. I should just turn this off." She reaches into her bag and powers down the phone.

Stavros comes by with an iced coffee for Mia and a Budweiser for me and leaves another awkward pause in his wake.

"So," I begin.

"So," Mia repeats.

"So, you have a usual at this place. This like your regular spot?"

"I come for the spanakopita and nagging. It's close to campus, so I used to come here a lot."

Used to? For like the twentieth time tonight, I do the math. It's been three years since Mia left for Juilliard. That would make her a senior this fall. But she's playing Carnegie Hall? She has management? I'm suddenly wishing I'd paid more attention to that article.

"Why not anymore?" My frustration echoes through the din.

Mia's face prickles up to attention, and a little caterpillar of anxiety bunches up above the bridge of her nose. "What?" she says quickly.

"Aren't you *still* in school?"

"Oh, that," she says, relief unfurling her brow. "I should've explained it before. I graduated in the spring. Juilliard has a three-year-degree option for . . ."

"Virtuosos." I mean it as a compliment, but my annoyance at not having the baseball card on Mia Hall— the stats, highlights, career bests—turns it bitter.

"Gifted students," Mia corrects, almost apologetically. "I graduated early so I can start touring sooner. Now, actually. It all starts now."

"Oh."

We sit there in an awkward silence until Stavros arrives with the food. I didn't think I was hungry when we ordered, but as soon as I smell the burger, my stomach starts rumbling. I realize all I've eaten today is a couple of hot dogs. Stavros lays down a bunch of plates in front of Mia, a salad, a spinach pie, French fries, rice pudding.

"*That's* your regular?" I ask.

"I told you. I haven't eaten in two days. And you know how I much I can put away. Or knew, I mean . . ."

"You need anything, Maestro, you just holler."

"Thanks, Stavros."

After he leaves, we both kill a few minutes drowning our fries and the conversation in ketchup.

"So . . ." I begin.

"So . . ." she repeats. Then: "How's everyone. The rest of the band?"

"Good."

"Where are they tonight?"

"London. Or on their way."

Mia cocks her head to the side. "I thought you said you were going tomorrow."

"Yeah, well, I had to tie up some loose ends. Logistics and all that. So I'm here an extra day."

"Well that's lucky."

"*What?*"

"I mean . . . fortunate, because otherwise we wouldn't have bumped into each other."

I look at her. Is she serious? Ten minutes ago she

looked like she was about to have a coronary at the mere *possibility* of being my girlfriend, and now she's saying it's lucky I stalked her tonight. Or is this merely the polite small talk portion of the evening?

"And how's Liz? Is she still with Sarah?"

Oh, it is the small talk interlude. "Oh yeah, going strong. They want to get married and have this big debate about whether to do it in a legal state like Iowa or wait for Oregon to legalize. All that trouble to tie the knot." I shake my head in disbelief.

"What, you don't want to get married?" she asks, a hint of challenge in her voice.

It's actually kind of hard to return her stare, but I force myself. "Never," I say.

"Oh," she says, sounding almost relieved.

Don't panic, Mia. I wasn't gonna propose.

"And you? Still in Oregon?" she asks.

"Nope. I'm in L.A. now."

"Another rain refugee flees south."

"Yeah, something like that." No need to tell her how the novelty of being able to eat dinner outside in February wore off quickly, and how now the lack of seasons seems fundamentally wrong. I'm like the opposite of those people who need to sit under sunlamps in the gloom of winter. In the middle of L.A.'s sunny non-winter, I need to sit in a dark closet to feel right. "I moved my parents down, too. The heat's better for my dad's arthritis."

"Yeah, Gramps's arthritis is pretty bad, too. In his hip."

Arthritis? Could this be any more like a Christmas-card update: *And Billy finished swimming lessons, and Todd knocked up his girlfriend, and Aunt Louise had her bunions removed.*

"Oh, that sucks," I say.

"You know how he is. He's all stoic about it. In fact, he and Gran are gearing up to do a lot of traveling to visit me on the road, got themselves new passports. Gran even found a horticulture student to look after her orchids when she's away."

"So how are your gran's orchids?" I ask. *Excellent. We've moved on to flowers now.*

"Still winning prizes, so I guess they must be doing well." Mia looks down. "I haven't seen her greenhouse in a while. I haven't been back there since I came out here."

I'm both surprised by this—and not. It's like I knew it already, even though I thought that once I skipped town, Mia might return. Once again, I've overestimated my importance.

"You should look them up sometime," she says. "They'd be so happy to hear from you, to hear about how well you're doing."

"How *well* I'm doing?"

When I look up at her, she's peering at me from under a waterfall of hair, shaking her head in wonder. "Yeah, Adam, how *amazing* you're doing. I mean, you did it. You're a rock star!"

Rock star. The words are so full of smoke and mirrors that it's impossible to find a real person behind them. But I *am* a rock star. I have the bank account of a rock star and the platinum records of a rock star and the girlfriend of a rock star. But I fucking hate that term, and hearing Mia pin it on me ups the level of my loathing to a new stratosphere.

"Do you have any pictures of the rest of the band?" she asks. "On your phone or something?"

"Yeah, pictures. I have a ton on my phone, but it's back at the hotel." Total bullshit but she'll never know. And if it's pictures she wants, I can just get her a copy of *Spin* at a corner newsstand.

"I have some pictures. Mine are actual paper pictures because my phone is so ancient. I think I have some of Gran and Gramps, and oh, a great one of Henry and Willow. They brought their kids to visit me at the Marlboro Festival last summer," she tells me. "Beatrix, or Trixie as they call her, remember their little girl? She's five now. And they had another baby, a little boy, Theo, named for Teddy."

At the mention of Teddy's name, my gut seizes up. In the calculus of feelings, you never really know how one person's absence will affect you more than another's. I loved Mia's parents, but I could somehow accept their deaths. They'd gone too soon, but in the right order—parent before child—though, not, I supposed, from the perspective of Mia's grandparents. But somehow I *still* can't wrap my head around Teddy staying eight years old forever. Every year I get older, I think about how old Teddy would be, too. He'd be almost twelve now, and I see him in the face of every zitty adolescent boy who comes to our shows or begs an autograph.

I never told Mia about how much losing Teddy gutted me back when we were together, so there's no way I'm gonna tell her now. I've lost my right to discuss such things. I've relinquished—or been relieved of—my seat at the Hall family table.

"I took the picture last summer, so it's a little old, but you get the idea of how everyone looks."

"Oh, that's okay."

But Mia's already rooting through her bag. "Henry still looks the same, like an overgrown kid. Where is my wallet?" She heaves the bag onto the table.

"I don't want to see your pictures!" My voice is as sharp as ice cracking, as loud as a parent's reprimand.

Mia stops her digging. "Oh. Okay." She looks chastened, slapped down. She zips her bag and slides it back into the booth, and in the process, knocks over my bottle of beer. She starts frantically grabbing at napkins from the dispenser to sop up the brew, like there's battery acid leaking over the table. "Damn!" she says.

"It's no big deal."

"It is. I've made a huge mess," Mia says breathlessly.

"You got most of it. Just call your buddy over and he'll get the rest."

She continues to clean maniacally until she's emptied the napkin dispenser and used up every dry paper product in the vicinity. She balls up the soiled napkins and I think she's about to go at the tabletop with her bare arm, and I'm watching the whole thing, slightly perplexed. Until Mia runs out of gas. She stops, hangs her head. Then she looks up at me with those eyes of hers. "I'm sorry."

I know the cool thing to do is say it's okay, it's no big deal, I didn't even get beer on me. But all of a sudden I'm not sure we're talking about beer, and if we're *not* talking about beer, if Mia's issuing some stealth apology . . .

What are you sorry about, Mia?

Even if I could bring myself to ask that—which I

can't—she's jumping out of the booth and running to-ward the bathroom to clean the beer off herself like she's Lady Macbeth.

She's gone for a while, and as I wait the ambiguity she left in the booth curdles its way into the deepest part of me. Because I've imagined a lot of scenarios over the last three years. Most of them versions of this all being some kind of Huge Mistake, a giant misunderstanding. And a lot of my fantasies involve the ways in which Mia grovels for my forgiveness. Apologizes for returning my love with the cruelty of her silence. For acting as though two years of life—those two years of *our* lives—amount to nothing.

But I always stop short of the fantasy of her apolo-gizing for leaving. Because even though she might not know it, she just did what I told her she could do.

NINE

There were signs. Probably more of them than I ever caught, even after the fact. But I missed them all. Maybe because I wasn't looking for them. I was too busy checking over my shoulder at the fire I'd just come through to pay much attention to the thousand-foot cliff looming in front of me.

When Mia had decided to go to Juilliard that fall, and when by late that spring it became clear that she'd be able to, I'd said I'd go with her to New York. She'd just given me this look, *no way*. "That was never on the table before," she said, "so why should it be now?"

Because before you were a whole person but now you don't have a spleen. Or parents. Because New York might swallow you alive, I'd thought. I didn't say anything.

"It's time for both of us to get back to our lives," she continued. I'd only been at the university part-time before but had just stopped going after the accident and now had a term's worth of incompletes. Mia hadn't been back to school, either. She'd missed too much of it, and now she worked with a tutor to finish up her senior year classes so she could graduate and go to Juilliard on time. It was more going through the motions. Her teachers would pass her even if she never turned in another assignment.

"And what about the band?" she asked. "I know they're all waiting on you." Also true. Just before the accident, we'd recorded a self-titled record on Smiling Simon, a Seattle-based independent label. The album had come out at the beginning of the summer, and even though we hadn't toured to support it, the CD had been selling up a storm, getting tons of play on college radio stations. As a result, Shooting Star now had major labels circling, all interested in signing a band that existed only in theory. "Your poor guitar is practically dying of neglect," she said with a sad smile. It hadn't been out of its case since our aborted opening act for Bikini.

So, I agreed to the long-distance thing. In part

because there was no arguing with Mia. In part because I really didn't want to quit Shooting Star. But also, I was kind of cocky about the distance. I mean, before I'd been worried about what the continental divide would do to us. But *now*? What the hell could twenty-five hundred miles do to us now? And besides, Kim had accepted a spot at NYU, a few miles downtown from Juilliard. She'd keep an eye on Mia.

Except, then Kim made a last-minute change and switched to Brandeis in Boston. I was furious about this. After the accident, we frequently had little chats about Mia's progress and passed along pertinent info to her grandparents. We kept our talks secret, knowing Mia would've killed us had she thought we were conspiring. But Kim and I, we were like co-captains of Team Mia. If I couldn't move to New York with Mia, I felt Kim had a responsibility to stay near her.

I stewed about this for a while until one hot July night about a month before she and Mia were due to leave. Kim had come over to Mia's grandparents house to watch DVDs with us. Mia had gone to bed early so it was just the two of us finishing some pretentious foreign movie. Kim kept trying to talk to me about Mia, how well she was doing, and was jabbering over the film like a noisy parrot. I finally told her to shut up. Her eyes narrowed and she started gathering her stuff. "I know what you're upset about and it's not this lame movie, so why don't you just yell at me about it already and get it over with," she said. Then she'd burst out crying. I'd never seen Kim cry, full-on like this, not even at the memorial service, so I'd immediately felt like crap and apologized and sort of awkwardly hugged her.

After she'd finished sniveling, she'd dried her eyes and explained how Mia had made her choose Brandeis. "I mean, it's where I really want to go. After so long in Goyoregon, I really wanted to be at a Jewish school, but NYU was fine, and New York is plenty Jewish. But, she was fierce on this. She said she didn't want 'any more babysitting.' Those were her exact words. She swore that if I went to NYU, she'd know it was because we'd hatched a plan to keep an eye on her. She said she'd cut ties with me. I told her I didn't believe her, but she had a look in her eye I'd never seen. She was serious. So I did it. Do you know how many strings I had to pull to get my spot back this late in the game? Plus, I lost my tuition deposit at NYU. But whatever, it made Mia happy and not a lot does these days." Kim smiled ruefully. "So I'm not sure why it's making me feel so miserable. Guilt, I guess. Religious hazard." Then she'd started crying again.

Pretty loud sign. I guess I had my fingers in my ears.

But the end, when it finally came, was quiet.

Mia went to New York. I moved back to the House of Rock. I went back to school. The world didn't end. For the first couple of weeks, Mia and I sent each other these epic emails. Hers were all about New York, her classes, music, school. Mine were all about our record-label meetings. Liz had scheduled a bunch of gigs for us around Thanksgiving—and we had some serious practicing to do before then, given that I hadn't picked up a guitar in months—but, at Mike's insistence, we were seeing to business first. We were traveling to Seattle and L.A. and meeting label execs. Some A&R guys from New York were coming out to Oregon to see us. I told Mia about the promises they made, how each of them said they'd hone our sound and launch us to superstardom. All of us in the band tried to keep it in check, but it was hard not to inhale their stardust.

Mia and I also had a phone call check-in every night before she went to bed. She was usually pretty wiped so the conversations were short; a chance to hear one another's voice, to say *I love you* in real time.

One night about three weeks into the semester, I was a little late calling because we were meeting one of the A&R reps for dinner at Le Pigeon in Portland and everything ran a little late. When my call went to voice mail, I figured she'd already gone to sleep.

But the next day, there was no email from her. "Sorry I was late. U pissed @ me?" I texted her.

"No," she texted right back. And I was relieved.

But that night, I called on time, and that call went right to voice mail. And the next day, the email from Mia was a terse two sentences, something about orchestra getting very intense. So I justified it. Things were starting to heat up. She was at Juilliard, after all. Her cello didn't have WiFi. And this was Mia, the girl known to practice eight hours a day.

But then I started calling at different times, waking up early so I could get her before classes, calling during her dinnertime. And my calls kept going to voice mail, never getting returned. She didn't return my texts either. I was still getting emails, but not every day, and even though *my* emails were full of increasingly desperate questions—"Why aren't you picking up your cell?" "Did you lose it? Are you okay?"—her responses glossed right over everything. She just claimed to be busy.

I decided to go visit her grandparents. I'd pretty much lived with them for five months while Mia was recovering and had promised to visit frequently but I'd reneged on that. I found it hard to be in that drafty old house with its photo gallery of ghosts—a wedding portrait of Denny and Kat, a gut-wrenching shot of twelve-year-old Mia reading to Teddy on her lap—without Mia beside me. But with Mia's contact dwindling, I needed answers.

The first time I went that fall, Mia's grandmother talked my ear off about the state of her garden and then went out to her greenhouse, leaving me to sit in the kitchen with her grandfather. He brewed us a strong pot of coffee. We didn't say much, so all you could hear was the crackling of the woodstove. He just looked at me in that quiet sad way that made me inexplicably want to kneel at the foot of his chair and put my head in his lap.

I went back a couple more times, even after Mia had cut off contact with me completely, and it was always like that. I felt kind of bad pretending that I was there on social calls when really I was hoping for some news, some explanation. No, what I was *really* hoping for was not to be the odd man out. I wanted them to say: "Mia has stopped calling us. Has she been in touch with you?" But, of course, that never happened because that never *would* happen.

The thing was, I didn't need any confirmation from Mia's grandparents. I knew from that second night when my call went to voice mail, that it was the end of the line for me.

Because hadn't I told her? Hadn't I stood over her

body and promised her that I'd do anything if she stayed, even if it meant letting her go? The fact that she'd been in a coma when I'd said this, hadn't woken up for another three days, that neither of us had ever mentioned what I'd said—that seemed almost irrelevant. I'd brought this on myself.

The thing I can't wrap my head around is *how* she did it. I've never dumped a girl with such brutality. Even back when I did the groupie thing, I'd always escort the girl du jour out of my hotel room or limo or whatever, give her a chaste kiss on the cheek and a "Thanks, that was a lot of fun," or something with a similar note of finality in it. And that was a *groupie*. Mia and I had been together for more than two years, and yes, it was a high-school romance, but it was still the kind of romance where I thought we were trying to find a way to make it forever, the kind that, had we met five years later and had she not been some cello prodigy and had I not been in a band on the rise—or had our lives not been ripped apart by all this—I was pretty sure it would've been.

I've come to realize there's a world of difference between knowing something happened, even knowing why it happened, and believing it. Because when she cut off contact, yeah, I *knew* what had happened. But it took me a long, long time to believe it.

Some days, I *still* don't quite believe it.

TEN

After we leave the diner, I start to feel nervous. Because we bumped into each other. We did the polite thing and stuck around to catch up, so what's left except our good-byes? But I'm not ready for that. I'm pretty sure there's not going to be another postscript with Mia, and I'm gonna have to live on the fumes of tonight for the rest of my life, so I'd like a little more to show for it than parking lots and arthritis and aborted apologies.

Which is why every block we walk that Mia doesn't hail a cab or make excuses and say good night feels like a stay of execution. In the sound of my footsteps slapping against the pavement, I can almost hear the word, *reprieve, reprieve,* echo through the city streets.

We walk in silence down a much-quieter, much-scummier stretch of Ninth Avenue. Underneath a dank overpass, a bunch of homeless guys camp out. One asks for some spare change. I toss him a ten. A bus goes by, blasting a cloud of diesel exhaust.

Mia points across the street. "That's the Port Authority Bus Terminal," she says.

I just nod, not sure if we're going to discuss bus stations with the same amount of detail we did parking lots, or if she's planning on sending me away.

"There's a bowling alley inside," she tells me.

"In the bus station?"

"Crazy right?!" Mia exclaims, suddenly all animated. "I couldn't believe it when I found it either. I was coming home from visiting Kim in Boston late one night and got lost on the way out and there it was. It reminded me of Easter egg hunts. Do you remember how Teddy and I used to get about those?"

I remember how *Mia* used to get. She'd been a sucker for any holiday that had a candy association—especially making it fun for Teddy. One Easter she'd painstakingly hand-colored hard-boiled eggs and hidden them all over the yard for Teddy's hunt the next morning. But then it poured all night and all her colorful eggs had turned a mottled gray. Mia had been tearfully disappointed, but Teddy had practically peed himself with excitement—the eggs, he declared, weren't Easter eggs; they were *dinosaur* eggs.

"Yeah, I remember," I say.

"Everyone loves New York City for all these different reasons. The culture. The mix of people. The pace. The food. But for me, it's like one epic Easter egg hunt. You're always finding these little surprises around every corner. Like that garden. Like a bowling alley in a giant bus depot. You know—" She stops.

"What?"

She shakes her head. "You probably have something going tonight. A club. An entourage to meet."

I roll my eyes. "I don't do entourage, Mia." It comes out harder than I intended.

"I didn't mean it as an insult. I just assumed all rock stars, celebrities, traveled with packs."

"Stop assuming. I'm still me." *Sort of.*

She looks surprised. "Okay. So you don't have anywhere you need to be?"

I shake my head.

"It's late. Do you need to get to sleep?"

"I don't do much of that these days. I can sleep on the plane."

"So . . ." Mia kicks away a piece of trash with her

toe, and I realize *she's still nervous.* "Let's go on an urban Easter egg hunt." She pauses, searches my face to see if I know what she's talking about, and of course I know exactly what she's talking about. "I'll show you all the secret corners of the city that I love so much."

"Why?" I ask her. And then as soon as I ask the question, I want to kick myself. *You got your reprieve, now shut up!* But part of me does want to know. If I'm unclear why I went to her concert tonight, I'm thoroughly confused as to why she called me to her, why I'm still here.

"Because I'd like to show you," she says simply. I stare at her, waiting for her to elaborate. Her brows knit as she tries to explain. Then she seems to give up. She just shrugs. After a minute she tries again: "Also, I'm not exactly leaving New York, but I sort of am. I go to Japan tomorrow to do two concerts there and then one in Korea. And after that I come back to New York for a week and then I really start touring. I'll be on the road for maybe forty weeks a year, so . . ."

"Not much time for egg hunting?"

"Something like that."

"So this would be like your farewell tour?" *Of New York? Of me?*

A little late for me.

"That's one way of looking at it, I suppose," Mia replies.

I pause, as though I'm actually considering this, as though I'm weighing my options, as though the RSVP to her invitation is in question. Then I shrug, put on a good show, "Sure, why not?"

But I'm still a little iffy about the bus station, so I put on my shades and cap before we go inside. Mia leads me through an orange-tiled hall, the aroma of pine disinfectant not quite masking the smell of piss, and up a series of escalators, past shuttered newsstands and fast-food restaurants, up more escalators to a neon sign blaring LEISURE TIME BOWL.

"Here we are," she says shyly, proudly. "After I found it by accident, I made a habit of peeking in any time I was in the station. And then I started coming here just to hang out. Sometimes I sit at the bar and order nachos and watch people bowl."

"Why not bowl yourself?"

Mia tilts her head to the side, then taps her elbow.

Ahh, her elbow. Her Achilles' heel. One of the few parts of her body that, it seemed, hadn't been hurt in the accident, hadn't been encased in plaster or put together with pins or stitches or touched by skin grafts. But when she'd started playing cello again in that mad attempt to catch up with herself, her elbow had started to hurt. X-rays were taken. MRIs done. The doctors couldn't find anything wrong, told her it might be a bad bruise or a contused nerve, and suggested she ease off the practicing, which had set Mia off. She said if she couldn't play, she had nothing left. *What about me?* I remember thinking, but never saying. Anyhow, she'd ignored the doctors and played through the pain and either it had gotten better or she'd gotten used to it.

"I tried to get some people from Juilliard to come down a few times, but they weren't into it. But it doesn't matter," she tells me. "It's the *place* I love. How it's totally secreted away up here. I don't need to bowl to appreciate it."

So your Garden-of-Eden boyfriend is too highbrow for greasy diners and bowling alleys, huh?

Mia and I used to go bowling, sometimes the two of us, other times with her whole family. Kat and Denny had been big bowlers, part of Denny's whole retro thing. Even Teddy could hit an eighty. *Like it or not, Mia Hall, you have a bit of grunge twined into your DNA, thanks to your family. And, maybe, thanks to me.*

"We could go bowling now," I suggest.

Mia smiles at the offer. Then taps her elbow again. She shakes her head.

"You don't have to bowl," I explain. "I'll bowl. You can watch. Just for you to get the whole effect. Or I can even bowl for both of us. It seems like you should have one game here. This being your farewell tour."

"You'd do that for me?" And it's the surprise in her voice that gets to me.

"Yeah, why not? I haven't been bowling in ages." This isn't entirely true. Bryn and I went bowling a few months ago for some charity thing. We paid twenty thousand bucks to rent a lane for an hour for some worthy cause and then we didn't even bowl; just drank champagne while Bryn schmoozed. I mean who drinks champagne at a bowling alley?

Inside Leisure Time, it smells like beer—and wax and hot dogs and shoe disinfectant. It's what a bowling alley should smell like. The lanes are full of an unusually unattractive grouping of New Yorkers who actually seem to be bowling for the sake of bowling. They don't look twice at us; they don't even look once at us. I book us a lane and rent us each a pair of shoes. Full treatment here.

Mia's practically giddy as she tries hers on, doing a little soft-shoe as she selects a ladies' pink eight-pounder for me to bowl with on her behalf.

"What about names?" Mia asks.

Back in the day, we always went for musicians; she'd choose an old-school punk female singer and I'd pick a male classical musician. Joan and Frederic. Or Debbie and Ludwig.

"You pick," I say, because I'm not exactly sure how

much of the past we're supposed to be reliving. Until I see the names she inputs. And then I almost fall over. *Kat* and *Denny*.

When she sees my expression she looks embarrassed. "They liked to bowl, too," she hastily explains, quickly changing the names to Pat and Lenny. "How's that?" she asks a little too cheerfully

Two letters away from morbid, I think. My hand is shaking again as I step up to the lane with "Pat's" pink ball, which might explain why I only knock down eight pins. Mia doesn't care. She squeals with delight. "A spare will be mine," she yells. Then catches her outburst and looks down at her feet. "Thanks for renting me the shoes. Nice touch."

"No problem."

"How come nobody recognizes you here?" she asks.

"It's a context thing."

"Maybe you can take off your sunglasses. It's kind of hard talking to you in them."

I forgot that I still had them on and feel stupid for it, and stupid for having to wear them in the first place. I take them off.

"Better," Mia says. "I don't get why classical musicians think bowling is white trash. It's so fun."

I don't know why this little Juilliard-snobs-versus-the-rest-of-us should make me feel a little digging thrill, but it does. I knock down the remaining two of Mia's pins. She cheers, loudly.

"Did you like it? Juilliard?" I ask. "Was it everything you thought it'd be?"

"No," she says, and again, I feel this strange sense of victory. Until she elaborates. "It was more."

"Oh."

"Didn't start out that way, though. It was pretty rocky at first."

"That's not surprising, you know, all things considered."

"That was the problem. 'All things considered.' Too many things considered. When I first got there, it was like everywhere else; people were very considerate. My roommate was so considerate that she couldn't look at me without crying."

The Over-Empathizer—her I remember. I got cut off a few weeks into her.

"All my roommates were drama queens. I changed so many times the first year before I finally moved out of the dorms. Do you know I've lived in eleven different places here? I think that must be some kind of record."

"Consider it practice for being on the road."

"Do you like being on the road?"

"No."

"Really? Getting to see all those different countries. I would've thought you'd love that."

"All I get to see is the hotel and the venue and the blur of the countryside from the window of a tour bus."

"Don't you *ever* sightsee?"

The band does. They go out on these private VIP tours, hit the Rome Colosseum before it's open to the public and things like that. I could tag along, but it would mean going with the band, so I just wind up holed up in my hotel. "There's not usually time," I lie. "So you were saying, you had roommate issues."

"Yeah," Mia continues. "Sympathy overload. It was like that with everyone, including the faculty, who were all kind of nervous around me, when it should've been the opposite. It's kind of a rite of passage when you first take orchestra to have your playing deconstructed—basically picked apart—in front of everyone. And it happened to everybody. Except me. It was like I was invisible. Nobody dared critique me. And trust me, it wasn't because my playing was so great."

"Maybe it was," I say. I edge closer, dry my hands over the blower.

"No. It wasn't. One of the courses you have to take when you first start is String Quartet Survey. And one of the profs is this guy Lemsky. He's a bigwig in the department. Russian. Imagine every cruel stereotype you can think of, that's him. Mean, shriveled-up little man. Straight out of Dostoyevsky. My dad would've loved him. After a few weeks, I get called into his office. This is not usually a happy sign.

"He's sitting behind this messy wooden desk, with papers and sheet music piled high. And he starts telling me about his family. Jews in the Ukraine. Lived through pogroms. Then through World War II. Then he says, 'Everyone has hardship in their life. Everyone has pain. The faculty here will coddle you because of what you went through. I, however, am of the opinion if we do that, that car crash might as well have killed you, too, because we will smother your talent. Do you want us to do that?'

"And, I didn't know how to respond, so I just stood there. And then he *yelled* at me: '*Do you? Do you want us to smother you?*' And I manage to eke out a 'no.' And he says, 'Good.' Then he picks up his baton and sort of flicks me out with it."

I can think of places I'd like to stick that guy's baton. I grab my ball and hurl it down the lane. It hits the pin formation with a satisfying thwack; the pins go flying in every direction, like little humans fleeing Godzilla. When I get back to Mia, I'm calmer.

"Nice one," she says at the same time I say, "Your professor sounds like a dick!"

"True, he's not the most socially graced. And I was freaked out at the time, but looking back I think that was one of the most important days of my life. Because he was the first person who didn't just give me a pass."

I turn, glad to have a reason to walk away from her so she can't see the look on my face. I throw her pink ball down the lane, but the torque is off and it veers to the right. I get seven down and the remaining three are split. I only pick off one more on my next go. To even things up, I purposely blow *my* next frame, knocking down six pins.

"So, a few days later, in orchestra," Mia continues, "my glissando gets taken apart, and not very kindly." She grins, awash in happy memories of her humiliation.

"Nothing like a public flogging."

"Right!? It was great. It was like the best therapy in the world."

I look at her. "Therapy" was once a forbidden word. Mia had been assigned a grief counselor in the hospital and rehab but had refused to continue seeing anyone once she'd come home, something Kim and I had argued against. But Mia had claimed that talking about her dead family an hour a week wasn't therapeutic.

"Once that happened, it was like everyone else on the

faculty relaxed around me," she tells me. "Lemsky rode me extra hard. No time off. No life that wasn't cello. Summers I played festivals. Aspen. Then Marlboro. Then Lemsky and Ernesto both pushed me to audition for the Young Concert Artists program, which was insane. It makes getting into Juilliard look like a cakewalk. But I did it. And I got in. That's why I was at Carnegie tonight. Twenty-year-olds don't normally play recitals at Zankel Hall. And that's just thrown all these doors wide open. I have management now. I have agents interested in me. And that's why Lemsky pushed for early graduation. He said I was ready to start touring, though I don't know if he's right."

"From what I heard tonight, he's right."

Her face is suddenly so eager, so young, it almost hurts. "Do you really think so? I've been playing recitals and festivals, but this will be different. This will be me on my own, or soloing for a few nights with an orchestra or a quartet or a chamber music ensemble." She shakes her head. "Some days I think I should just find a permanent position in an orchestra, have some continuity. Like you have with the band. It has to be such a comfort to always be with Liz, Mike, and Fitzy." The stage changes, but the players stay the same.

I think of the band, on an airplane as we speak, speeding across the Atlantic—an ocean, the least of the things, dividing us now. And then I think of Mia, of the way she played the Dvořák, of what all the people in the theater were saying after she left the stage. "No, you shouldn't do that. That would be a waste of your talent."

"Now *you* sound like Lemsky."

"Great."

Mia laughs. "Oh, I know he comes across as such a hard-ass, but I suspect deep down he's doing this because he thinks by giving me a shot at a career, he'll help fill some void."

Mia stops and turns to me, her eyes dead on mine, searching, reaching. "But he doesn't have to give me the career. That's not what fills the void. You understand that, right? You always understood that."

Suddenly, all the shit from the day comes ricocheting back—Vanessa and Bryn and the bump watches and *Shuffle* and the looming sixty-seven days of separate hotels and awkward silences and playing shows with a band behind me that no longer has my back.

And it's like, Mia, don't you get it? The *music* is the void. And you're the reason why.

ELEVEN

Shooting Star had always been a band with a code—feelings first, business second—so I hadn't given the band much thought, hadn't considered their feelings, or their resentments, about my extended leave. I figured they'd get my absence without my having to explain.

After I came out of my haze and wrote those first ten songs, I called Liz, who organized a band dinner/meeting. During dinner, we sat around the Club Table—so named because Liz had taken this fugly 1970s wooden dining table we'd found on the curb and covered it with band flyers and about a thousand layers of lacquer to resemble the inside of a club. First, I apologized for going MIA. Then I pulled out my laptop and played them recordings of the new stuff I'd been writing. Liz's and Fitzy's eyes went wide. They dangled vegetable lasagna in front of their mouths as they listened to track after track: "Bridge," "Dust," "Stitch," "Roulette," "Animate."

"Dude, we thought you were just packing it in, working some crap-ass job and pining, but you've been *productive*," Fitzy exclaimed. "This shit rocks."

Liz nodded. "It does. And it's beautiful, too. It must have been cathartic," she said, reaching over to squeeze my hand. "I'd love to read the lyrics. Do you have them on your computer?"

"Scrawled on paper at home. I'll transcribe them and email them to you."

"Home? Isn't this home?" Liz asked. "Your room is an untouched museum. Why don't you move back?"

"Not much to move. Unless you sold my stuff."

"We tried. Too dusty. No takers," Fitzy said. "We've been using your bed as a hat rack, though." Fitzy shot me a wiseass grin. I'd made the mistake of telling him how I'd thought I was turning into my dead grandfather, with all his weird superstitions, like his vehement belief that hats on beds bring bad luck.

"Don't worry, we'll burn sage," Liz said. Clearly Fitzy had alerted the media.

"So, what, that's it?" Mike said, tapping his nails against my laptop.

"Dude, that's ten songs," Fitzy said, a piece of spinach in his giant grin. "Ten insanely good songs. That's practically an album. We already have enough to go into the studio."

"Those are just the ones that are done," I interrupted. "I've got at least ten more coming. I don't know what's going on, but they're just kinda flowing out of me right now, like they're already written and recorded and someone just pressed *play*. I'm getting it all out as fast I can."

"Obey the muse," Liz said. "She's a fickle mistress."

"I'm not talking about the songs," Mike said. "We don't even know if there will be any album. If any of the labels will still want us. We had all this forward momentum and he basically killed it."

"He didn't kill anything," Liz said. "For one, it's only been a few months, and second of all, our Smiling Simon album has been ripping up the indie charts, getting tons of play on the college stations. And I've been working the college angle pretty well," Liz continued, "with interviews and all, to keep the embers burning."

"And dude, 'Perfect World' has even crossed over; it's getting play on satellite radio stations," Fitzy said. "I'm sure all those A&R guys will be happy to see us, shitting bricks to hear this."

"You don't know," Mike said. "They have their trends. Quotas. The outfits they want. And my point is, he"—he jabbed a finger at me—"ditches the band without a word and just waltzes back like it's no big deal."

Mike had a point, but it wasn't like I held anyone back. "Look, I'm sorry. We all go off the cliff sometimes. But you could've replaced me if you'd wanted to. Gotten a new guitar player and your major-label deal."

By the quick look that passed among the three of them, I could see that this option had been discussed, and likely vetoed by Liz. Shooting Star was a democratic outfit; we'd always made decisions together. But when it came down to it, the band was Liz's. She started it and recruited me to play guitar after seeing me play around town. Then she'd lassoed Fitzy and Mike, so ultimately a personnel change would've been her call. Maybe this was why Mike had started playing gigs with another drummer under the name of Ranch Hand.

"Mike, I don't get what you want out of this," Fitzy said. "Do you want a box of chocolates? Do you want Adam to get you a nice bouquet to say sorry?"

"Piss off, Fitz," Mike said.

"I'll buy you flowers," I offered. "Yellow roses. I believe those symbolize friendship. Whatever it takes, I'll do what I'm told."

"Will that make it good?" Fitzy continued. "Because what the fuck, man? We have these amazing songs. I wish I'd written those songs. But Adam did. He came through. And we have him back. So maybe now we can get back to making kick-ass music and see where it takes us. And maybe, you know, let our kid get a little joy back in his life. So, dude. Bygones."

Mike's worries turned out to be unfounded. Some of the major labels that had been courting us in the fall had cooled on us, but a handful were still interested, and when we sent them the demos of the songs that would become *Collateral Damage* they went ballistic, and we were signed and in the studio with Gus before we knew it.

And for a while, things were good. Fitzy and Liz were both right. Recording *Collateral Damage* was cathartic. And there was joy. Working with Gus was intense; he brought out the noise in us, told us not to be scared of our raw power, and we all ran with it. And it was cool being up in Seattle recording and staying in a corporate apartment and feeling like The Shit. Everything seemed good.

Not long after the record came out, the tour started. A five-month slog through North America, Europe, and Asia that, at the outset, seemed like the most exciting thing in the world. And in the beginning, it was. But it was also grueling. And soon I was tired all the time. And lonely. There was a lot of empty time in which to miss her. I kind of holed away in my hotel rooms, the backs of tour buses. I pushed everyone away. Even Liz. Especially Liz. She wasn't stupid; she knew what was going on—and why. And she wasn't some fragile flower, either. She kept after me. So I burrowed, until, I guess, she got tired of trying to dig me out.

As the tour went on, the album just started going haywire. Platinum. Then double-platinum. The tour dates sold out, so our promoters added additional ones to meet demand. The merchandising deals were everywhere. Shooting Star T-shirts, caps, posters, stickers, even a special-edition Shooting Star telescope. Suddenly, the press was all over us. Interviews all the time, which was flattering at first. People cared enough about us to read what we had to say.

But a weird thing started to happen in interviews. The reporter would sit the band down together, ask some perfunctory questions to us all, and then turn the microphone or camera on me. And I tried to open it up to the rest of the band. That's when reporters started requesting interviews with just me, a request I uniformly turned down, until it suddenly became impossible for us to do interviews any other way.

About four months into the tour, we were in Rome. *Rolling Stone* had sent a reporter to spend a few days with us. One night, after a show, we were closing the hotel bar. It was a pretty mellow scene and we were sitting around, decompressing, pounding grappa. But then the reporter starts firing away with all these heavy-duty questions. All to me. I mean, there were about a dozen of us in there—me, Liz, Fitzy, Mike, Aldous, some roadies, some groupies—but this guy was acting like I was the only person in the room. "Adam, do you see *Collateral Damage* as having a single narrative? If so, can you elaborate on it?" "Adam, do think this record represents your growth as a songwriter?" "Adam, you've mentioned in other interviews you don't want to go down 'that dark rock star path,' but how do you keep from suffocating on your own fumes?"

Mike just lost it. "You hijacked the band!" he screamed at me, like it was just the two of us in a room, like there wasn't a reporter right there. "This isn't just the Adam Wilde Show, you know. We're a band. A unit. There are four of us. Or did you forget that, on your way down the 'dark rock star path?'"

Mike turned to the reporter. "You wanna know

about the illustrious Adam Wilde? I've got some choice details. Like our rock star over here has to do this crazy voodoo shit before each show and is such a prima donna that if you whistle backstage before a show he has a tantrum because of the bad luck—"

"Mike, come on," Liz interrupted sharply. "All artists have their rituals."

The reporter, meanwhile, was scribbling away, eating all this up until Aldous diplomatically said that everyone was tired and shooed everyone but the band out of the bar and tried to get me and Mike to make nice. But then Mike just let loose for round two of insults, telling me what a spotlight-hogging asshole I'd become. I looked over at Liz to come to my defense again, but she was staring intently at her drink. So I turned to Fitzy, but he just shook his head. "I never thought I'd be the one to say this, but grow up, you two." Then he left. I looked pleadingly at Liz. She looked sympathetic, but tired. "Mike, you were out of line in there," she said flatly. But then she turned to me and shook her head. "But, Adam, come on. You've got to try to see it from his perspective. From *all* of ours. It's tough to be big about this, especially when you've retreated from us. I get why you have, but that doesn't make it any easier."

All of them—they were all against me. I waved my hands in surrender. I ran out of the bar, strangely close to tears. In the lobby, this Italian model named Rafaella, who'd been hanging with us, was waiting for a taxi. She smiled when she saw me. When her taxi came, she gestured with her head, inviting me inside. And I went. The next day, I checked into a different hotel from the band.

The story hit RollingStone.com almost immediately and the tabloids a few days later. Our label freaked, as did our tour promoters, all of whom warned of the various forms of hell there would be to pay if we didn't honor our concert commitments. Aldous flew in a professional mediator to talk to me and Mike. She was useless. Her genius idea, a legacy that continues to this day, is what Fitzy refers to as "The Divorce." I would continue to stay at one hotel for the remainder of the tour, the rest of the band at another. And our publicists decided it was safer to keep me and Mike separate in interviews, so now reporters often talk to me solo. Yeah, those changes have helped a lot!

When I got back from the *Collateral Damage* tour, I almost quit the band. I moved out of the house I'd been sharing with Fitzy in Portland and into my own place. I avoided those guys. I was angry, but also ashamed. I wasn't sure how, but I'd clearly ruined everything. I might've just let the run end there, but Liz stopped by my new place one afternoon and asked me to just give it a few months' breathing space and see how I felt. "Anyone would be going a little nuts after the couple years we've had, especially the couple of years you've had," she'd said, which was about as much as we acknowledged Mia. "I'm not asking you to do anything. I'm just asking you to *not* do anything and see how you feel in a few months."

Then the album started winning all these awards, and then I met Bryn and moved to L.A. and didn't have to deal with them much, so I just wound up getting sucked in for another round.

Bryn's the only person who knows how close to the edge that tour pushed me, and how badly I've been dreading this upcoming one. "Cut them loose," is her solution. She thinks I have some sort of guilt complex, coming from humble origins and all, and that's why I won't go solo. "Look, I get it. It's hard to accept that you deserve the acclaim, but you do. You write all the songs and most of the music and that's why you get all the attention," she tells me. "*You're* the talent! Not just some pretty face. If this were a movie, you'd be the twenty-million-dollar star and they'd be the supporting players, but instead you all get an equal split," she says. "You don't need them. Especially with all the grief they give you."

But it's not about the money. It never has been. And

going solo doesn't seem like much of a solution. It would just be out of the frying pan and into the fire. And there'd still be touring to contend with, the thought of which has been making me physically sick.

"Why don't you call Dr. Weisbluth?" Bryn suggested on the phone from Toronto, where she was wrapping her latest film. Weisbluth's the psychopharmacologist the label had hooked me up with a few months earlier. "See if he can give you something a little stronger. And when you get back, we need to have a sit-down with Brooke and seriously talk about you going solo. But you *have* to get through this tour. You'll blow your reputation otherwise."

There are worse things to blow than your reputation, aren't there? That's what I thought. But I didn't say it. I just called Weisbluth, got some more scripts, and steeled myself for the tour. I guess Bryn understood, like I understood, like everyone who knew me understood, that in spite of his bad-boy rep, Adam Wilde does as he's told.

TWELVE

There's a piece of lead where my heart should beat
Doctor said too dangerous to take out
You'd better just leave it be
Body grew back around it, a miracle, praise be
Now, if only I could get through airport security

"BULLET"

COLLATERAL DAMAGE, TRACK 12

Mia doesn't tell me what the next destination is. Says because it's her secret New York tour, it should be a secret and then proceeds to lead me out of Port Authority down, down, down into a warren of subway tunnels.

And I follow her. Even though I don't like secrets, even though I think that Mia and I have *enough* secrets between the two of us at this point, and even though the subway is like the culmination of all my fears. Enclosed spaces. Lots of people. No escape. I sort of mention this to her, but she throws back what I said earlier in the bowling alley about context. "Who's going to be expecting Adam Wilde on the subway at three in the morning? Without an entourage?" She gives me a joking smile. "Besides, it should be dead at this hour. And in my New York, I always take the train."

When we reach the Times Square subway station, the place is so crowded that it might as well be five P.M. on a Thursday. My warning bell starts to ping. Even more so once we get to the thronged platform. I stiffen and back toward one of the pillars. Mia gives me a look. "This is a bad idea," I mumble, but my worries are drowned out by the oncoming train.

"The trains don't run often at night, so it must be that everyone's been waiting for a while," Mia shouts over the clatter. "But here comes one now, so look, everything's fine."

When we get on the N, we both see that Mia's wrong. The car's packed with people. Drunk people.

I feel the itchiness of eyes on me. I know I'm out of pills, but I need a cigarette. *Now.* I reach for my pack.

"You can't smoke on the train," Mia whispers.

"I need to."

"It's illegal."

"I don't care." If I get arrested, at least I'd be in the safety of police custody.

Suddenly, she goes all Vulcan. "If the purpose is to not call attention to yourself, don't you think that perhaps lighting up is counterproductive?" She pulls me into a corner. "It's fine," she croons, and I half expect her to caress my neck like she used to do when I'd get tense. "We'll just hang out here. If it doesn't empty out at Thirty-fourth Street, we'll get off."

At Thirty-fourth, a bunch of people do get off, and I feel a little better. At Fourteenth more people get off. But then suddenly at Canal, our car fills up with a group of hipsters. I angle myself into the far end of the train, near the conductor's booth, so my back is to the riders.

It's hard for most people to understand how freaked out I get by large crowds in small contained spaces now. I think it would be hard for the me of three years ago to understand. But that me never had the experience of minding his own business at a small record shop in Minneapolis when one guy recognized me and shouted out my name and it was like watching popcorn kernels in hot oil: First one went, then another, then an explosion of them, until all these sedate record-store slackers suddenly became a mob, surrounding me, then tackling me. I couldn't breathe. I couldn't move.

It sucks because I like the fans when I meet them individually, I do. But get a group of them together and this swarm instinct takes over and they seem to forget that you're a mere mortal: flesh and bone, bruisable and scareable.

But we seem okay in the corner. Until I make the fatal mistake of doing just one final check over my shoulder to make sure no one's looking at me. And in that little quarter second, it happens. I catch someone's eye. I feel the recognition ignite like a match. I can almost smell the phosphorus in the air. Then everything seems to happen in slow motion. First, I hear it. It goes unnaturally quiet. And then there's a low buzz as the news travels. I hear my name, in stage whispers, move across the noisy train. I see elbows nudged. Cell phones reached for, bags grabbed, forces rallied, legs shuffling. None of this takes longer than a few seconds, but it's always agonizing, like the moments when a first punch is thrown but hasn't yet connected. One guy with a beard is preparing to step out of his seat, opening his mouth to call my name. I know he means me no harm, but once he outs me, the whole train will be on me. Thirty seconds till all hell breaks loose.

I grab Mia's arm and yank.

"Oww!"

I have the door between subway cars open and we're pushing into the next car.

"What are you doing?" she says, flailing behind me

I'm not listening. I'm pulling her into another car then another until the train slows into a station and then I'm tugging her out of the train, onto the platform, up

x

the stairs, taking them two at a time, some part of my brain vaguely warning me that I'm being too rough but the other part not giving a shit. Once up on the street, I pull her along for a few blocks until I'm sure no one is following us. Then I stop.

"Are you *trying* to get us killed?" she yells.

I feel a bolt of guilt shoot through me. But I throw the bolt right back at her.

"Well, what about you? Are you trying to get me attacked by a mob?"

I look down and realize that I'm still holding her hand. Mia looks, too. I let go.

"What mob, Adam?" she asks softly.

She's talking to me like I'm a crazy person now. Just like Aldous talks to me when I have one of my panic attacks. But at least Aldous would never accuse me of fantasizing a fan attack. He's seen it happen too many times.

"I got recognized down there," I mutter, walking away from her.

Mia hesitates for a second, then skitters to catch up. "Nobody knew it was you."

Her ignorance—the *luxury* of that ignorance!

"The whole car knew it was me."

"What are you talking about, Adam?"

"What am I talking about? I'm talking about having

photographers camped out in front of my house. I'm talking about not having gone record shopping in almost two years. I'm talking about not being able to take a walk without feeling like a deer on the opening day of hunting season. I'm talking about every time I have a cold, it showing up in a tabloid as a coke habit."

I look at her there in the shadows of the shut-down city, her hair falling onto her face, and I can see her trying to figure out if I've lost it. And I have to fight the urge to take her by the shoulders and slam her against a shuttered building until we feel the vibrations ringing through both of us. Because I suddenly want to hear her bones rattle. I want to feel the softness of her flesh give, to hear her gasp as my hip bone jams into her. I want to yank her head back until her neck is exposed. I want to rip my hands through her hair until her breath is labored. I want to make her cry and then lick up the tears. And then I want to take my mouth to hers, to devour her alive, to transmit all the things she can't understand.

"This is bullshit! Where the hell are you taking me anyway?" The adrenaline thrumming through me turns my voice into a growl.

Mia looks taken aback. "I told you. I'm taking you to my secret New York haunts."

"Yeah, well, I'm a little over secrets. Do you mind

telling me where we're going. Is that too much to fucking ask?"

"Christ, Adam, when did you become such a . . ."

Egomaniac? Asshole? Narcissist? I could fill in the
blank with a million words. They've all been said before.

". . . guy?" Mia finishes.

For a second, I almost laugh. *Guy*? That's the best
she's got? It reminds me of the story my parents tell
about me, how when I was a little kid and would get
angry, I'd get so worked up and then curse them out by
going "You, you, you . . . *piston*!" like it was the worst
thing ever.

But then I remember something else, an old conversation Mia and I had late one night. She and Kim had this
habit of categorizing everything into diametric catego-
ries, and Mia was always announcing a new one. One
day she told me that they'd decided that my gender was
divvied into two neat piles—Men and Guys. Basically,
all the saints of the world: Men. The jerks, the players,
the wet T-shirt contest aficionados? They were Guys.
Back then, I was a Man.

So I'm a Guy now? A Guy! I allow my hurt to show
for half a second. Mia's looking at me with confusion,
but not remembering a thing.

Whoever said that the past isn't dead had it backward.
It's the future that's already dead, already played out.

This whole night has been a mistake. It's not going to let me rewind. Or unmake the mistakes I've made. Or the promises I've made. Or have her back. Or have me back.

Something's changed in Mia's face. Some type of recognition has clicked on. Because she's explaining herself, how she called me a guy because guys always need to know the plan, the directions, and how she's taking me on the Staten Island Ferry, which isn't really a secret but it's something few Manhattanites ever do, which is a shame because there's this amazing view of the Statue of Liberty and on top of that, the ferry is free and nothing in New York is free, but if I'm worried about crowds we can forget it, but we can also just check it out and if it's not empty—and she's pretty sure it will be this time of night—we can get right back off before it leaves.

And I have no idea if she remembered that conversation about the Man/Guy distinction or not, but it doesn't really matter anymore. Because she's right. I *am* a Guy now. And I can peg the precise night I turned into one.

THIRTEEN

The groupies started showing up right away. Or maybe they'd always been there and I just hadn't noticed. But as soon as we started touring, they were buzzing about like hummingbirds dipping their beaks into spring flowers.

One of the first things we did after we signed with the label was hire Aldous to manage us. *Collateral Damage* was due to come out in September, and the label planned a modest tour in the late fall, but Aldous had different ideas.

"You guys need to get your sea legs back," Aldous

said when we finished mixing the album. "You need to get back on the road."

So right as the album came out, Aldous booked us a series of ten tour dates up and down the West Coast, in clubs we'd played in before, to reconnect with our fan base—or to remind them that we still existed—and to get comfortable playing in front of an audience again.

The label rented us a nice Econoline van, tricked out with a bed in the back, and a trailer to haul our gear, but other than that when we set out, it didn't feel that different from the shows we'd always played.

It was completely different.

For one, right away and for whatever reason, "Animate" was breaking out as a hit single. Even over the course of the two-week tour, its momentum was building and as that happened, you could feel it in every consecutive show we played. They went from well-attended to packed to sold-out to lines around the corner to fire marshals showing up. All in a matter of two weeks.

And the energy. It was like a live wire, like everyone at the shows knew we were right there on the verge and they wanted to be a part of it, a part of our history. It was like we were all in on this secret together. Maybe that's why these were the best, most frenetic, rocking shows we'd ever played—tons of stage diving and people shouting along to the songs, even though nobody had heard any of our new stuff before. And I felt pretty good, pretty vindicated because even though it was just a matter of pure luck that things had gone this way, *I* hadn't blown it for the band after all.

The groupies just seemed part of this wave of energy, this growing swell of fandom. At first, I didn't even think of them as groupies because a lot of the girls I'd known vaguely from the scene. Except whereas before they'd been friendly, now they were brazen in their flirting. After one of our first shows in San Francisco, this hipster chick named Viv who I'd known for a few years came backstage. She had glossy black hair and wiry arms covered in a daisy chain of tattoos. She gave me a huge hug and then a kiss on the mouth. She hung by my side all night long, her hand resting on the small of my back.

At that point, I'd been out of commission for well over a year. Mia and I, well, she'd been in the hospital, then in rehab, and even if she hadn't been covered in stitches, plaster, and pressure bandages, there was no way. All those fantasies about sexy hospital sponge baths are a joke; there is no place *less* of a turn-on than a hospital. The smell alone is one of putrefaction—the opposite of desire.

When she'd come home, it had been to a downstairs room that had been her gran's sewing room, which we'd turned into Mia's bedroom. I'd slept on a nearby couch in the living room. There were spare rooms on the second floor, but Mia, who was still walking with a cane, couldn't handle the stairs at first, and I hadn't wanted to be even that far away.

Even though I was spending every night at Mia's, I'd never officially moved out of the House of Rock, and one night, a few months after Mia had come back to her grandparents', she'd suggested we go there. After dinner with Liz and Sarah, Mia had tugged me up to my room. The minute the door clicked shut behind us, she'd pounced on me, kissing me with her mouth wide open, like she was trying to swallow me whole. I'd been taken aback at first, freaked out by this sudden ardor, worried that it was going to hurt her, and also, not really wanting to look at the stubbly red scar on her thigh where the skin had been taken for her graft or to bang against the snakeskin-like scar on her other leg, even though she kept that one covered with a pressure bandage.

But as she'd kissed me, my body had begun waking up to her, and with it, my mind had gone, too. We'd laid down on my futon. But then, right as things had gotten going, she'd started crying. I couldn't tell at first because the little sobs had sounded just the same as the little moans she'd been giving off moments before. But soon, they'd grown in intensity, something awful and animal coming from deep within her. I'd asked if I'd hurt her, but she'd said that wasn't it and asked me to leave the room. When she'd come out fully dressed, she'd asked to go home.

She'd tried to start things up with me once more after that. A summer night a few weeks before she'd left for Juilliard. Her grandparents had gone away to visit her aunt Diane, so we'd had the house to ourselves for the night, and Mia had suggested we sleep in one of the up-stairs bedrooms since by then the stairs were no longer a problem for her. It had been hot. We'd opened the win-dows and kicked off the antique quilt and just gotten under the sheet. I remember feeling all self-conscious, sharing a bed with her after all that time. So I'd grabbed a book for myself and propped up a row of pillows for Mia to bolster her leg against, like she liked to at night.

"I'm not ready to sleep," she'd said, running a finger down my bare arm.

She'd leaned in to kiss me. Not the usual dry peck on the lips but a deep, rich, exploring kiss. I'd started to kiss her back. But then I'd remembered that night at the House of Rock, the sound of her animal keening, the look of fear in her eyes when she'd come out of the bed-room. *No way* was I sending her down that wormhole again. No way was *I* going down that wormhole again.

That night in San Francisco, though, with Viv's hand playing on the small of my back, I was raring to go. I spent the night with her at her apartment, and she came with me the next morning to have breakfast with the band before we took off for our next stop. "Call me next time you're in town," she whispered in my ear as we parted ways.

"Back on the horse, my man," Fitzy said, high-fiving me as we piloted the van south.

"Yeah, congratulations," Liz said, a little sadly. "Just don't rub it in." Sarah had recently finished law school and was working for a human rights organization. No more dropping everything to be Liz's plus-one on tours anymore.

"Just because you and Mikey are all tied down, don't come sobbing to us," Fitzy said. "Tour time is playtime, right, Wilde Man?"

"Wilde Man?" Liz asked. "Is that how it's gonna be?"

"No," I said.

"Hey, if the name fits . . ." Fitzy said. "Good thing I hit Fred Meyer for the economy box of condoms before we left."

In L.A., there was another girl waiting. And in San Diego, another. But none of it felt skeevy. Ellie, the girl in L.A. was an old friend, and Laina, the one in San Diego, was a grad student—smart and sexy and older. Nobody had any illusions that these flings were leading to grand romance.

It wasn't until our second-to-last gig that I met a girl whose name I never did catch. I noticed her from the stage. She locked eyes on me the entire set and wouldn't stop staring. It was weirding me out but also building me up. I mean she was practically undressing me with her eyes. You couldn't help but feel powerful and turned on, and it felt good to be so obviously wanted again.

Our label was throwing us a CD-release party after the show, invitation only. I didn't expect to see her there. But after a few hours, there she was, striding up to me in an outfit that was half hooker, half super-model: skirt cut up to there, boots that could double as military-grade weaponry.

She marched right up to me and announced in a not-too-quiet voice: "I've come all the way from England to fuck you." And with that, she grabbed my hand and led me out the door and to her hotel room.

The next morning was awkward like none of the morning afters had been. I did a walk of shame to the bathroom, quickly dressed and tried to slip out, but she was right there, packed and ready to go. "What are you doing?" I asked.

"Coming with you?" she said, as though it was obvious.

"Coming with me where?"

"To Portland, love."

Portland was our last show and a sort of homecoming as we'd all be basing there now. Not in a communal House of Rock anymore. Liz and Sarah were getting their own place. Mike was moving in with his girlfriend. And Fitzy and I were renting a house together. But we were all still in the same area, within walking distance to one another and the rehearsal space we now rented.

"We're in a van. Not a tour bus," I told her, looking down at my Converse. "And Portland's the last show, a kind of friends-and-family thing. You shouldn't come." *And you are not my love.*

She frowned and I'd slunk out the door, thinking that was the last of it. But when I showed up to sound check in Portland, she was there, waiting for me in the Satyricon. I told her to leave, not very nicely. It was along the lines of: *There's a name for this and it's called stalking.* I was a dick, I know, but I was tired. I'd asked her not to come. And she was freaking me out in a big way. Not just her. Four girls in two weeks was doing my head in. I needed to be alone.

"Piss off, Adam. You're not even a bloody rock star

yet, so stop acting like such a self-important wanker. And you weren't even that good." This she shouted in front of everyone.

So I had the roadies throw her out. She left screaming insults about me, my sexual prowess, my ego.

"Wilde Man, indeed," Liz said, raising an eyebrow.

"Yeah," I said, feeling like the opposite of a wild man, actually wanting to sneak into a room and hide. I didn't know it yet, but once the real tour started—the one our label sent us on after the album went haywire, a five-month slog of sold-out shows and groupies galore—all I'd wanted to do was hide. Given my isolationist tendencies, you'd think I'd have learned to stay away from the freebie affection on such constant offer. But after shows, I craved connection. I craved skin—the taste of another woman's sweat. If it couldn't be *hers*, well, then anyone's would do . . . for a few hours. But I'd learned one lesson—no more overnight guests.

So, that night in Seattle may have been the first time I became a guy. But it wasn't the last.

FOURTEEN

The boogeyman sleeps on your side of the bed
Whispers in my ear: "Better off dead."
Fills my dreams with sirens and lights of regret
Kisses me gently when I wake up in a sweat

"BOO!"

COLLATERAL DAMAGE, TRACK 3

I go with Mia to the ferry anyway. Because what else am I going to do? Throw a tantrum because she hasn't kept an up-to-date catalog of every conversation we've ever had. *It's called moving on.*

And she's right about the ferry being dead. At four thirty in the morning, not a lot of demand for Staten Island. There are maybe a dozen people sprawled out in the downstairs deck. One trio of late-night stragglers is sacked out on a bench, rehashing the evening, but as we pass them, one of the girls lifts her head and stares at me. Then she asks her friend, "Dude, is that Adam Wilde?"

The friend laughs. "Yeah. And next to him is Britney Spears. Why the hell would Adam Wilde be on the Staten Island Ferry?"

I'm asking myself the same question.

But this is apparently one of Mia's things, and this is her farewell-to-New-York-even-though-I'm-not-actually-leaving tour. So I follow her upstairs to the bow of the boat near the railing.

As we pull away from New York, the skyline recedes behind us and the Hudson River opens up to one side, the harbor to the other. It's peaceful out here on the water, quiet except for a pair of hopeful seagulls following in our wake, squawking for food, I guess, or maybe just some company in the night. I start to relax in spite of myself.

And after a few minutes, we're close to the Statue of Liberty. She's all spotlit in the night, and her torch is also illuminated, like there's really a flame in there, welcoming the huddled masses. *Yo, lady, here I am.*

I've never been to the Statue of Liberty. Too many crowds. Aldous once invited me on a private helicopter tour, but I don't do choppers. But now that she's right here, I can see why this is on Mia's list. In pictures, the statue always looks kind of grim, determined, But up close, she's softer. She has a look on her face, like she knows something you don't.

"You're smiling," Mia says to me.

And I realize I am. Maybe it's being granted a special pass to do something I thought was off-limits. Or maybe the statue's look is contagious.

"It's nice," Mia says. "I haven't seen it in a while."

"It's funny," I reply, "because I was just thinking about her." I gesture toward the statue. "It's like she has some kind of secret. The secret to life."

Mia looks up. "Yeah. I see what you mean."

I blow air out my lips. "*I* could really use that secret."

Mia tilts her head out over the railing. "Yeah? So ask her for it."

"Ask her?"

"She's right there. No one's here. No tourists crawling around her feet like little ants. Ask her for her secret."

"I'm not going to ask her."

"You want me to do it? I will, but it's your question, so I think you should do the honors."

"You make a habit of talking to statues?"

"Yes. And pigeons. Now, are you going to ask?"

I look at Mia. She's got her arms crossed across her chest, a little impatient. I turn back to the railing. "Um. Statue? Oh, Statue of Liberty," I call out quietly. No one is around, but this is still really embarrassing.

"Louder," Mia prods.

What the hell. "Hey, excuse me," I call out, "what's your secret?"

We both cock our ears out over the water, as though we expect an answer to come racing back.

"What did she say?" Mia asks.

"Liberty."

"Liberty," Mia repeats, nodding in agreement. "No, wait, I think there's more. Hang on." She leans out over the railing, widening her eyes. "*Hmm. Hmm.* Aha." She turns to me. "Apparently, she isn't wearing any underwear under her robes, and with the bay breeze, it provides a certain *frisson.*"

"Lady Liberty's going commando," I say. "That is *so* French!"

Mia cracks up at that. "Do you think she ever flashes the tourists?"

"No way! Why do you think she has that private little look on her face? All those red-state puritans coming by the boatload, never once suspecting that Old Libs hasn't got panties on. She's probably sporting a Brazilian."

"Okay, I need to lose that visual," Mia groans. "And might I remind you that we're from a red state— sort of."

"Oregon's a divided state," I reply. "Rednecks to the east, hippies to the west."

"Speaking of hippies, and going commando . . ."

"Oh, no. Now that's a visual I really don't need."

"Mammary Liberation Day!" Mia crows, referring to some sixties holdover in our town. Once a year a bunch of women spend the day topless to protest the inequity that it's legal for men to go shirtless, but not women. They do it in the summer, but Oregon being Oregon, half the time, it's still freezing, so there was a lot of aging puckered flesh. Mia's mom had always threatened to march; her dad had always bribed her with a dinner out at a fancy restaurant not to.

"Keep Your Class B Misdemeanor off My B Cups," Mia says, quoting one of the movement's more ridiculous slogans between gasps of laughter. "That makes no sense. If you're baring your boobs, why a bra?"

"Sense? It was some stoner hippie idea. And you're looking for logic?"

"Mammary Liberation Day," Mia says, wiping away the tears. "Good old Oregon! That was a lifetime ago."

And it was. So the remark shouldn't feel like a slap. But it does. "How come you never went back?" I ask. It's not really Oregon's abandonment I want explained, but it seems safer to hide under the big green blanket of our state.

"Why should I?" Mia asks, keeping her gaze steady over the water.

"I don't know. The people there."

"The people there can come here."

"To visit them. Your family. At the . . ." *Oh, shit, what am I saying?*

"You mean the graves?"

I just nod.

"Actually, they're the reason I don't go back."

I nod my head. "Too painful."

Mia laughs. A real and genuine laugh, a sound about as expected as a car alarm in a rain forest. "No, it's not like that at all." She shakes her head. "Do you honestly think that where you're buried has any bearing on where your spirit lives?"

Where your spirit lives?

"Do you want to know where my family's spirits live?"

I suddenly feel like I'm talking to a spirit. The ghost of rational Mia.

"They're here," she says, tapping her chest. "And here," she says, touching her temple. "I hear them all the time."

I have no idea what to say. Were we not just making fun of all the New Agey hippie types in our town two minutes ago?

But Mia's not kidding anymore. She frowns deeply, swivels away. "Never mind."

"No. I'm sorry."

"No, I get it. I sound like a Rainbow Warrior. A freak. A Looney Tune."

"Actually, you sound like your gran."

She stares at me. "If I tell you, you'll call the guys with the straitjackets."

"I left my phone at the hotel."

"Right."

"Also, we're on a boat."

"Good point."

"And if by chance they do show up, I'll just offer myself up. So, what, do they, like, haunt you?"

She takes a deep breath and her shoulders slump as if she's setting down a heavy load. She beckons me over to one of the empty benches. I sit down next to her.

"'Haunt' is not the right word for it. Haunt makes it sound bad, unwelcome. But I do hear them. All the time."

"Oh."

"Not just hear their voices, like the memory of them," she goes on. "I can hear them talk to me. Like now. In real time. About my life."

I must give her a weird look, because she blushes. "I know. I hear dead people. But it's not like *that*. Like remember that crazy homeless woman who used to wander around the college campus claiming she heard voices broadcast to her shopping cart?" I nod. Mia stops for a minute.

"At least I don't *think* it's like that," she says. "Maybe it is. Maybe I am nuts and just don't think I am because crazy people never think they're crazy, right? But I really *do* hear them. Whether it's some kind of angel force like Gran believes, and they're up in some heaven on a direct line to me, or whether it's just the them I've stored inside me, I don't know. And I don't know if it even matters. What matters is that they're with me. All the time. And I *know* I sound like a crazy person, mumbling to myself sometimes, but I'm just talking to Mom about what skirt to buy or to Dad about a recital I'm nervous about or to Teddy about a movie I've seen.

"And I can hear them answer me. Like they're right there in the room with me. Like they never really went away. And here's what's really weird: I couldn't hear them back in Oregon. After the accident, it was like their voices were receding. I thought I was going to totally lose the ability to remember what they even sounded like. But once I got away, I could hear them all the time. That's why I don't want to go back. Well, one of the reasons. I'm scared I'll lose the connection, so to speak."

"Can you hear them now?"

She pauses, listens, nods.

"What are they saying?"

"They're saying it's so good to see you, Adam."

I know she's sort of joking, but the thought that they can see me, keep tabs on me, know what I've done these last three years, it makes me actually shudder in the warm night.

Mia sees me shudder, looks down. "I know, it's crazy. It's why I've never told anyone this. Not Ernesto. Not even Kim."

No, I want to tell her. *You got it wrong. It's not crazy at all.* I think of all the voices that clatter around in my head, voices that I'm pretty sure are just some older, or younger, or just *better* versions of me. There have been times—when things have been really bleak—that I've tried to summon *her,* to have *her* answer me back, but it never works. I just get me. If I want her voice, I have to rely on memories. At least I have plenty of those.

I can't imagine what it would be like to have had her company in my head—the comfort that would've brought. To know that she's had *them* with her all this time, it makes me glad. It also makes me understand why, of the two of us, she seems like the sane one.

FIFTEEN

I'm pretty sure that when babies are born in Oregon, they leave the hospital with birth certificates—and teeny-tiny sleeping bags. Everyone in the state camps. The hippies and the rednecks. The hunters and the tree huggers. Rich people. Poor people. Even rock musicians. *Especially* rock musicians. Our band had perfected the art of punk-rock camping, throwing a bunch of crap into the van with, like, an hour's notice and just driving out into the mountains, where we'd drink beer, burn food, jam on our instruments around the campfire, and sack out under the open sky. Sometimes, on tour, back in the early hardscrabble days, we'd even camp as an alternative to crashing in another crowded, roach-infested rock 'n' roll house.

I don't know if it's because no matter where you live, the wilderness is never that far off, but it just seemed like everyone in Oregon camped.

Everyone, that was, except for Mia Hall.

"I sleep in beds," was what Mia told me the first time I invited her to go camping for a weekend. To which I'd offered to bring one of those blow-up air mattresses, but she'd still refused. Kat had overheard me trying to persuade Mia and had laughed.

"Good luck with that, Adam," she'd said. "Denny and I took Mia camping when she was a baby. We planned to spend a week at the coast, but she screamed for two days straight and we had to come home. She's allergic to camping."

"It's true," Mia had said.

"I'll go," Teddy had offered. "I only ever get to go camp in the backyard."

"Gramps takes you out every month," Denny had replied. "And I take you. You just don't get to go camping with all of us as a *family*." He'd given Mia a look. She'd just rolled her eyes back at him.

So it shocked me when Mia agreed to go camping. It was the summer before her senior year of high school and my first year of college, and we'd hardly seen each other. Things with the band had really started heating up, so I'd been touring for a lot of that summer, and Mia had been away at her band camp and then visiting relatives. She must've been really missing me. It was the only explanation I could imagine for her relenting.

I knew better than to rely on the punk-rock mode of camping. So I borrowed a tent. And one of those foam things to sleep on. And I packed a cooler full of food. I wanted to make everything okay, though to be honest, I wasn't really clear on why Mia was so averse to camping in the first place—she was not a prissy chick, not by a long shot; this was a girl who liked to play midnight basketball—so I had no idea if the creature comforts would help.

When I went to pick her up, her whole family came down to see us off, like we were heading off on a cross-country road trip instead of a twenty-four-hour jaunt. Kat waved me over.

"What'd you pack, for food?" she asked.

"Sandwiches. Fruit. For tonight, hamburgers, baked beans, s'mores. I'm trying for the authentic camping experience."

Kat nodded, all serious. "Good, though you might want to feed her the s'mores first if she gets cranky.

Also, I packed you some provisions." She handed me a half-gallon Ziploc. "In case of emergency, break glass."

"What's all this stuff?"

"Now and Laters. Starburst. Pixie Stix. If she gets too bitchy, just feed her this crap. As long as the sugar high is in effect, you and the wildlife should be safe."

"Well, thanks."

Kat shook her head "You're a braver man than I. Good luck."

"Yeah, you'll need it," Denny replied. Then he and Kat locked eyes for a second and started cracking up.

There were plenty of great camping spots within an hour's drive, but I wanted to take us somewhere a little more special, so I wound us deep into the mountains, to this place up an old logging road I'd been to a lot as a kid. When I pulled off the road, onto a dirt path, Mia asked: "Where's the campground?"

"Campgrounds are for tourists. We free camp."

"Free camp?" Her voice rose in alarm.

"Relax, Mia. My dad used to log around here. I know these roads. And if you're worried about showers and stuff—"

"I don't care about the showers."

"Good, because we have our own private pool." I turned off my car and showed Mia the spot. It was right alongside the river, where a small inlet of water pooled calm and crystal clear. The view in all directions was unfettered, nothing but pine trees and mountains, like a giant postcard advertising OREGON!

"It's pretty," Mia admitted, grudgingly.

"Wait till you see the view from the top of the ridge. You up for a walk?"

Mia nodded. I grabbed some sandwiches and waters and two packs of watermelon Now and Laters and we traipsed up the trail, hung out for a while, read our books under a tree. By the time we got back down, it was twilight.

"I'd better get the tent up," I said.

"You need some help?"

"No. You're the guest. You relax. Read your book or something."

"If you say so."

I dumped the borrowed tent pieces on the ground and started to hook up the poles. Except the tent was one of those newfangled ones, where all the poles are in one giant puzzle piece, not like the simple pup tents I'd grown up assembling. After half an hour, I was still struggling with it. The sun was dipping behind the mountains, and Mia had put down her book. She was watching me, a bemused little smile on her face.

"Enjoying this?" I asked, perspiring in the evening chill.

"Definitely. Had I known this was what it would be like, I would've agreed to come ages ago."

"I'm glad you find it so amusing."

"Oh, I do. But are you sure you wouldn't like some help? You'll need me to hold a flashlight if this takes much longer."

I sighed. Held my hands up in surrender. "I'm being bested by a piece of sporting goods."

"Does your opponent have instructions?"

"It probably did at some point."

She shook her head, stood up, grabbed the top of the tent. "Okay, you take this end. I'll do this end. I think the long part loops over the top here."

Ten minutes later we had the tent set up and staked down. I collected some rocks and some kindling for a fire pit and got a campfire going with the firewood I'd brought. I cooked us burgers in a pan over the fire and baked beans directly in the can.

"I'm impressed," Mia said.

"So you like camping?"

"I didn't say that," she said, but she was smiling.

It was only later, after we'd had dinner and s'mores and washed our dishes in the moonlit river and I'd played some guitar around the campfire as Mia sipped tea and chowed through a pack of Starburst, that I finally understood Mia's issue with camping.

It was maybe ten o'clock, but in camping time, that's like two in the morning. We got into our tent, snuggled into the double sleeping bag. I pulled Mia to me. "Wanna know the best part about camping?"

I felt her whole body tense up—but not in the good way. "What was that?" she whispered.

"What was what?"

"I heard something," she said.

"It was probably just an animal," I said.

She flicked on the flashlight. "How do you know that?"

I took the flashlight and shined it on her. Her eyes were huge. "You're scared?"

She looked down and—barely—nodded her head.

"The only thing you need to worry about out here is bears and they're only interested in the food, which is why we put it all away in the car," I reassured her.

"I'm not scared of bears," Mia said disdainfully.

"Then what is it?"

"I, I just feel like such a sitting target out here."

"Sitting target for who?"

"I don't know, people with guns. All those hunters."

"That's ridiculous. Half of Oregon hunts. My whole family hunts. They hunt animals, not campers."

"I know," she said in a small voice. "It's not really that, either. I just feel . . . defenseless. It's just, I don't know, the world feels so big when you're out in the wide open. It's like you don't have a place in it when you don't have a home."

"Your place is right here," I whispered, laying her down and hugging her close.

She snuggled into me. "I know." She sighed. "What a freak! The granddaughter of a retired Forest Service biologist who's scared of camping."

"That's just the half of it. You're a classical cellist whose parents are old punk rockers. You're a *total* freak. But you're *my* freak."

We lay there in silence for a while. Mia clicked off the flashlight and scooted closer to me. "Did you hunt as a kid?" she whispered. "I've never heard you mention it."

"I used to go out with my dad," I murmured back. Even though we were the only people within miles, something about the night demanded we speak in hushed tones. "He always said when I was twelve I'd get a rifle for my birthday and he'd teach me to shoot. But when I was maybe nine, I went out with some older cousins and one of them loaned me his rifle. And it must've been beginner's luck or something because I shot a rabbit. My cousins were all going crazy. Rabbits are small and quick and hard for even seasoned hunters to kill, and I'd hit one on my first try. They went to get it so we could bring it back to show everyone and maybe stuff it for a trophy. But when I saw it all bloody, I just started crying. Then I started screaming that we had to take it to a vet, but of course it was dead. I wouldn't let them bring it back. I made them bury it in the forest. When my dad heard, he told me that the point of hunting was to take some sustenance from the animal, whether we eat it or skin it or something, otherwise it was a waste of a life. But I think he knew I wasn't cut out for it because when I turned twelve, I didn't get a rifle; I got a guitar."

"You never told me that before," Mia said.

"Guess I didn't want to blow my punk-rock credibility."

"I would think that would cement it," she said.

"Nah. But I'm emocore all the way, so it works."

A warm silence hung in the tent. Outside, I could hear the low hoot of an owl echo in the night. Mia nudged me in the ribs. "You're such a softy!"

"This from the girl who's scared of camping!"

She chuckled. I pulled her closer to me, wanting to eradicate any distance between our bodies. I pushed her hair off her neck and nuzzled my face there. "Now you owe me an embarrassing story from your childhood," I murmured into her ear.

"All my embarrassing stories are still happening," she replied.

"There must be one I don't know."

She was silent for a while. Then she said: "Butterflies."

"Butterflies?"

"I was terrified of butterflies."

"What is it with you and nature?"

She shook with silent laughter. "I know," she said. "And can there be a less-threatening creature than a butterfly? They only live, like, two weeks. But I used to freak any time I saw one. My parents did everything they could to desensitize me: bought me books on butterflies, clothes with butterflies, put up butterfly posters in my room. But nothing worked."

"Were you like attacked by a gang of monarchs?" I asked.

"No," she said. "Gran had this theory behind my phobia. She said it was because one day I was going to have to go through a metamorphosis like a caterpillar transforming into a butterfly and that scared me, so butterflies scared me."

"That sounds like your gran. How'd you get over your fear?"

"I don't know. I just decided not to be scared of them anymore and then one day I wasn't."

"Fake it till you make it."

"Something like that."

"You could try that with camping."

"Do I have to?"

"Nah, but I'm glad you came."

She'd turned to face me. It was almost pitch-black in the tent but I could see her dark eyes shining. "Me too. But do we have to go to sleep? Can we just stay like this for a while?"

"All night long if you want. We'll tell our secrets to the dark."

"Okay."

"So let's hear another one of your irrational fears."

Mia grasped me by the arms and pulled herself in to my chest, like she was burrowing her body into mine. "I'm scared of losing you," she said in the faintest of voices.

I pushed her away so I could see her face and kissed the top of her forehead. "I said 'irrational' fears. Because that's not gonna happen."

"It still scares me," she murmured. But then she went on to list other random things that freaked her out and I did the same, and we kept whispering to each other, telling stories from our childhoods, deep, deep into the night until finally Mia forgot to be scared and fell asleep.

The weather turned cool a few weeks later, and that winter was when Mia had her accident. So that actually turned out to be the last time I went camping. But even if it weren't, I still think it would be the best trip of my life. Whenever I remember it, I just picture our tent, a little ship glowing in the night, the sounds of Mia's and my whispers escaping like musical notes, floating out on a moonlit sea.

SIXTEEN

You crossed the water, left me ashore
It killed me enough, but you wanted more
You blew up the bridge, a mad terrorist
Waved from your side, threw me a kiss
I started to follow but realized too late
There was nothing but air underneath my feet

"BRIDGE"
COLLATERAL DAMAGE, TRACK 4

Fingers of light are starting to pry open the night sky.
Soon the sun will rise and a new day will inarguably
begin. A day in which I'm leaving for London. And Mia
for Tokyo. I feel the countdown of the clock ticking like
a time bomb.

We're on the Brooklyn Bridge now, and though Mia
hasn't said so specifically, I feel like this must be the
last stop. I mean, we're leaving Manhattan—and not a
round-trip like our cruise out to Staten Island and back
was. And also, Mia has decided, I guess, that since she's

pulled some confessionals, it's my turn. About halfway across the bridge, she stops suddenly and turns to me.

"So what's up with you and the band?" she asks.

There's a warm wind blowing, but I suddenly feel cold. "What do you mean, 'what's up?'"

Mia shrugs. "Something's up. I can tell. You've hardly talked about them all night. You guys used to be inseparable, and now you don't even live in the same state. And why didn't you go to London together?"

"I told you, logistics."

"What was so important that they couldn't have waited one night for you?"

"I had to, to do some stuff. Go into the studio and lay down a few guitar tracks."

Mia eyes me skeptically. "But you're on tour for a new album. Why are you even recording?"

"A promo version of one of our singles. More of this," I say, frowning as I rub my fingers together in a money-money motion.

"But wouldn't you be recording together?"

I shake my head. "It doesn't really work like that anymore. And besides, I had to do an interview with *Shuffle*."

"An interview? Not with the band? Just with you? That's what I don't get."

I think back to the day before. To Vanessa LeGrande. And out of the blue, I'm recalling the lyrics to "Bridge," and wondering if maybe discussing this with Mia Hall above the dark waters of the East River isn't such a hot idea. At least it isn't Friday the thirteenth anymore.

"Yeah. That's kinda how it works these days, too," I say.

"Why do they only want just you? What do they want to know about?"

I really don't want to talk about this. But Mia's like a bloodhound, tracking a scent, and I know her well enough to know that I can either throw her a piece of bloody meat, or let her sniff her way to the real pile of stinking corpses. I go for the diversion.

"Actually, that part's kinda interesting. The reporter, she asked about you."

"What?" Mia swivels around to face me.

"She was interviewing me and asked about you. About us. About high school." The look of shock on Mia's face, I savor it. I think about what she said earlier, about her life in Oregon being a lifetime ago. *Well, maybe not* such *a lifetime ago!* "That's the first time that's happened. Kinda strange coincidence, all things considered."

"I don't believe in coincidences anymore."

"I didn't tell her anything, but she'd gotten a hold of

the old *Cougar* yearbook. The one with our picture—Groovy and the Geek."

Mia shakes her head. "Yeah, I *so* loved that nickname."

"Don't worry. I didn't say anything. And for good measure, I smashed her recorder. Destroyed all evidence."

"Not *all* the evidence." She stares at me. "The *Cougar* lives on. I'm sure Kim will be delighted to know her early work may turn up in a national magazine." She shakes her head and chuckles. "Once Kim gets you in her shutter, you're stuck forever. So it was pointless to destroy that reporter's recorder."

"I know. I just sort of lost it. She was this very provocative person, and she was trying to get a rise out of me with all these insults-disguised-as-compliments."

Mia nods knowingly. "I get that, too. It's the worst! 'I was fascinated by the Shostakovich you played tonight. So much more subdued than the Bach,' she says in a snooty voice. 'Translation: The Shostakovich sucked.'"

I can't imagine the Shostakovich ever sucking, but I won't deny us this common ground.

"So what did she want to know about me?"

"She had plans to do this big exposé, I guess, on what makes Shooting Star tick. And she went digging around our hometown and talked to people we went to high

school with. And they told her about us . . . about the
. . . about what we were. And about you and what
happened . . ." I trail off. I look down at the river, at a
passing barge, which, judging by its smell, is carrying
garbage.

"And what really happened?" Mia asks.

I'm not sure if this is a rhetorical question, so I force
my own voice into a jokey drawl. "Yeah, that's what I'm
still trying to figure out."

It occurs to me that this is maybe the most honest
thing I've said all night, but the way I've said it trans-
forms it into a lie.

"You know, my manager warned me that the accident might get a lot of attention as my profile went up,
but I didn't think that the connection to you would be
an issue. I mean, I did in the beginning. I sort of waited
for someone to look me up—ghosts of girlfriends past—
but I guess I wasn't interesting enough compared to
your other, um, attachments."

She thinks *that's* why none of the hacks have pestered
her, because she's not as interesting as Bryn, who I guess
she *does* know about. If only she knew how the band's
inner circle has bent over backward to keep her name
out of things, to not touch the bruise that blooms at the
mere mention of her. That right at this very moment
there are riders in interview contracts that dictate whole

swaths of forbidden conversational topics that, though they don't name her specifically, are all about obliterating her from the record. Protecting her. And me.

"I guess high school really is ancient history," she concludes.

Ancient history? Have you really relegated us to the trash heap of the Dumb High-School Romance? And if that's the case, why the hell can't I do the same?

"Yeah, well you plus me, we're like MTV plus Lifetime," I say, with as much jauntiness as I can muster. "In other words, shark bait."

She sighs. "Oh, well. I suppose even sharks have to eat."

"What's that supposed to mean?"

"It's just, I don't particularly want my family history dragged through the public eye, but if that's the price to be paid for doing what you love, I guess I'll pay it."

And we're back to this. The notion that music can make it all worthwhile—I'd *like* to believe. I just don't. I'm not even sure that I ever did. It isn't the *music* that makes me want to wake up every day and take another breath. I turn away from her toward the dark water below.

"What if it's not what you love?" I mumble, but my voice gets lost in the wind and the traffic. But at least I've said it out loud. I've done that much.

I need a cigarette. I lean against the railing and look uptown toward a trio of bridges. Mia comes to stand beside me as I'm fumbling to get my lighter to work.

"You should quit," she says, touching me gently on the shoulder.

For a second, I think she means the band. That she heard what I said before and is telling me to quit Shooting Star, leave the whole music industry. I keep waiting for someone to advise me to quit the music business, but no one ever does. Then I remember how earlier tonight, she told me the same thing, right before she bummed a cigarette. "It's not so easy," I say.

"Bullshit," Mia says with a self-righteousness that instantly recalls her mother, Kat, who wore her certitude like a beat-up leather jacket and who had a mouth on her that could make a roadie blush. "Quitting's not hard. *Deciding* to quit is hard. Once you make that mental leap, the rest is easy."

"Really? Was that how you quit me?"

And just like that, without thinking, without saying it in my head first, without arguing with myself for days, it's out there.

"So," she says, as if speaking to an audience under the bridge. "He finally says it."

"Was I not supposed to? Am I just supposed to let this whole night go without talking about what you did?"

"*No*," she says softly.

"So why? Why did you go? Was it because of the voices?"

She shakes her head. "It wasn't the voices."

"Then what? What was it?" I hear the desperation in my own voice now.

"It was lots of things. Like how you couldn't be yourself around me."

"What are you talking about?"

"You stopped talking to me."

"That's absurd, Mia. I talked to you all the time!"

"You talked to me, but you didn't. I could see you having these two-sided conversations. The things you wanted to say to me. And the words that actually came out."

I think of all the dual conversations I have. With everyone. Is *that* when it started? "Well, you weren't exactly easy to talk to," I shoot back. "Anything I said was the wrong thing."

She looks at me with a sad smile. "I know. It wasn't just you. It was you plus me. It was us."

I just shake my head. "It's not true."

"Yes it is. But don't feel bad. Everyone walked on eggshells around me. But with you, it was painful that you couldn't be real with me. I mean, you barely even touched me."

As if to reinforce the point, she places two fingers on the inside of my wrist. Were smoke to rise and the imprints of her two fingers branded onto me, I wouldn't be the least bit surprised. I have to pull away just to steady myself.

"You were healing," is my pathetic reply. "And if I recall, when we did try, you freaked."

"Once," she says. "Once."

"All I wanted was for you to be okay. All I wanted was to help you. I would've done *anything*."

She drops her chin to her chest. "Yes, I know. You wanted to rescue me."

"Damn, Mia. You say that like it's a bad thing."

She looks up at me. The sympathy is still in her eyes, but there's something else now, too: a fierceness; it slices up my anger and reconstitutes it as dread.

"You were so busy trying to be my savior that you left me all alone," she says. "I know you were trying to help, but it just felt, at the time, like you were pushing me away, keeping things from me for my own good and making me more of a victim. Ernesto says that people's good intentions can wind up putting us in boxes as confining as coffins."

"Ernesto? What the hell does he know about it?"

Mia traces the gap between the wooden boardwalk planks with her toe. "A lot, actually. His parents were killed when he was eight. He was raised by his grandparents."

I know what I'm supposed to feel is sympathy. But the rage just washes over me. "What, is there some *club*?" I ask, my voice starting to crack. "A grief club that I can't join?"

I expect her to tell me no. Or that I'm a member. After all, I lost them, too. Except even back then, it had been different, like there'd been a barrier. That's the thing you never expect about grieving, what a competition it is. Because no matter how important they'd been to me, no matter how *sorry* people told me they were, Denny and Kat and Teddy weren't my family, and suddenly that distinction had mattered.

Apparently, it still does. Because Mia stops and considers my question. "Maybe not a grief club. But a guilt club. From being left behind."

Oh, don't talk to me about guilt! My blood runs thick with it. On the bridge, now I feel tears coming. The only way to keep them at bay is to find the anger that's sustained me and push back with it. "But you could've at least told me," I say, my voice rising to a shout. "Instead of dropping me like a one-night stand, you could've had the decency to break up with me instead of leaving me wondering for three years. . . ."

"I didn't plan it," she says, her own pitch rising. "I

didn't get on that plane thinking we'd split up. You were *everything* to me. Even as it was happening, I didn't believe it was happening. But it was. Just being here, being away, it was all so much easier in a way I didn't anticipate. In a way I didn't think my life could be anymore. It was a huge relief."

I think of all the girls whose backs I couldn't wait to see in retreat. How once their sound and smell and voices were gone, I felt my whole body exhale. A lot of the time Bryn falls into this category. *That's how my absence felt to Mia?*

"I planned to tell you," she continues, the words coming out in a breathless jumble now, "but at first I was so confused. I didn't even know what was happening, only that I was feeling better *without* you and how could I explain that *to* you? And then time went by, you didn't call me, when you didn't pursue it, I just figured that you, *you* of all people, you understood. I knew I was being a chickenshit. But I thought . . ." Mia stumbles for a second then regains her composure. "I thought I was allowed that. And that you understood it. I mean you seemed to. You wrote: 'She says I have to pick: Choose you, or choose me. She's the last one standing.' I don't know. When I heard 'Roulette' I just thought you *did* understand. That you were angry, but you knew. I had to choose *me*."

"*That's* your excuse for dropping me without a word? There's cowardly, Mia. And then there's cruel! Is that who you've become?"

"Maybe it was who I needed to be for a while," she cries. "And I'm sorry. I know I should've contacted you. Should've explained. But you weren't all that accessible."

"Oh, bullshit, Mia. I'm inaccessible to most people. But you? Two phone calls and you could've tracked me down."

"It didn't feel that way," she said. "You were this . . ." she trails off, miming an explosion, the same as Vanessa LeGrande had done earlier in the day. "Phenomenon. Not a person anymore."

"That's such a load of crap and you should know it. And besides, that was more than a year after you left. *A year.* A year in which I was curled up into a ball of misery at my parents' house, Mia. Or did you forget that phone number, too?"

"No." Mia's voice is flat. "But I couldn't call you at first."

"Why?" I yell. "Why not?"

Mia faces me now. The wind is whipping her hair this way and that so she looks like some kind of mystical sorceress, beautiful, powerful, and scary at the same time. She shakes her head and starts to turn away.

Oh, no! We've come this far over the bridge. She can

blow the damn thing up if she wants to. But not with-out telling me everything. I grab her, turn her to face me. "Why not? Tell me. You owe me this!"

She looks at me, square in the eye. Taking aim. And then she pulls the trigger. "Because I hated you."

The wind, the noise, it all just goes quiet for a second, and I'm left with a dull ringing in my ear, like after a show, like after a heart monitor goes to flatline.

"Hated me? Why?"

"You made me stay." She says it quietly, and it almost gets lost in the wind and the traffic and I'm not sure I heard her. But then she repeats it louder this time. "You made me stay!"

And there it is. A hollow blown through my heart, confirming what some part of me has always known.

She knows.

The electricity in the air has changed; it's like you can smell the ions dancing. "I still wake up every single morning and for a second I forget that I don't have my family anymore," she tells me. "And then I remember. Do you know what that's like? Over and over again. It would've been so much easier . . ." And suddenly her calm facade cracks and she begins to cry.

"Please," I hold up my hands. "Please don't . . ."

"No, you're right. You have to let me say this, Adam! You have to hear it. It would've been easier to die. It's not that I want to be dead now. I don't. I have a lot in my life that I get satisfaction from, that I love. But some days, especially in the beginning, it was so hard. And I couldn't help but think that it would've been so much simpler to go with the rest of them. But you—you asked me to stay. You *begged* me to stay. You stood over me and you made a promise to me, as sacred as any vow. And I can understand why you're angry, but you can't blame me. You can't hate me for taking your word."

Mia's sobbing now. I'm wracked with shame because I brought her to this.

And suddenly, I get it. I understand why she summoned me to her at the theater, why she came after me once I left her dressing room. *This* is what the farewell tour is really all about—Mia completing the severance she began three years ago.

Letting go. Everyone talks about it like it's the easiest thing. Unfurl your fingers one by one until your hand is open. But my hand has been clenched into a fist for three years now; it's frozen shut. All of me is frozen shut. And about to shut down completely.

I stare down at the water. A minute ago it was calm and glassy but now it's like the river is opening up, churning, a violent whirlpool. It's that vortex, threatening to swallow me whole. I'm going to drown in it, with nobody, *nobody* in the murk with me.

I've blamed her for all of this, for leaving, for ruining me. And maybe that was the seed of it, but from that one little seed grew this tumor of a flowering plant. And *I'm* the one who nurtures it. I water it. I care for it. I nibble from its poison berries. I let it wrap around my neck, choking the air right out of me. I've done that. All by myself. All to myself.

I look at the river. It's like the waves are fifty feet high, snapping at me now, trying to pull me over the bridge into the waters below.

"I can't do this anymore!" I yell as the carnivorous waves come for me.

Again, I scream, *"I can't do this anymore!"* I'm yelling to the waves and to Liz and Fitzy and Mike and Aldous, to our record executives and to Bryn and Vanessa and the paparazzi and the girls in the U Mich sweatshirts and the scenesters on the subway and everyone who wants a piece of me when there aren't enough pieces to go around. But mostly I'm yelling it to myself.

"I CAN'T DO THIS ANYMORE!" I scream louder than I've ever screamed in my life, so loud my breath is knocking down trees in Manhattan, I'm sure of it. And as I battle with invisible waves and imaginary vortexes and demons that are all too real and of my own making, I actually feel something in my chest open, a feeling so intense it's like my heart's about to burst. And I just let it. I just let it out.

When I look up, the river is a river again. And my hands, which had been gripping the railing of the bridge so tight that my knuckles had gone white, have loosened.

Mia is walking away, walking toward the other end of the bridge. Without me.

I get it now.

I have to make good on my promise. To let her go. To really let her go. To let us both go.

SEVENTEEN

I started playing in my first band, Infinity 89, when I was fourteen years old. Our first show was at a house party near the college campus. All three of us in the band—me on guitar, my friend Nate on bass, and his older brother Jonah on drums—sucked. None of us had been playing for long, and after the gig we found out that Jonah had bribed the host of the party to let us play. It's a little-known fact that Adam Wilde's first foray into playing rock music in front of an audience might never have happened had Jonah Hamilton not pitched in for a keg.

The keg turned out to be the best thing about that show. We were so nervous that we turned the amps up too loud, creating a frenzy of feedback that made the neighbors complain, and then we overcompensated by playing so low that we couldn't hear one another's instruments.

What I could hear in the pauses between songs was the sound of the party: the din of beer bottles clinking, of mindless chatter, of people laughing, and, I swear, in the back room of the house, people watching *American Idol*. The point is, I could hear all this because our band was so crappy that no one bothered to acknowledge that we were playing. We weren't worth cheering. We were too bad to even boo. We were simply ignored. When we finished playing, the party carried on as if we'd never gone on.

We got better. Never great, but better. And never good enough to play anything but house parties. Then Jonah went off to college, and Nate and I were left without a drummer, and that was the end of Infinity 89.

Thus began my brief stint as a lone singer-songwriter about town, playing in coffeehouses, mostly. Doing the café circuit was marginally better than the house parties. With just me and a guitar, I didn't need to up the volume that much, and people in the audience were mostly respectful. But as I played, I was still distracted by the sounds of things other than the music: the hiss of the cappuccino maker, the intellectual college students' hushed conversations about Important Things, the giggles of girls. After the show, the giggles grew louder as the girls came up to me to talk, to ask me about my inspiration, to offer me mix CDs they'd made, and sometimes to offer other things.

One girl was different. She had ropy muscled arms and a fierce look in her eyes. The first time she spoke to me she said only: "You're wasted."

"Nope. Sober as a stone," I replied.

"Not that kind of wasted," she said, arching her pierced eyebrow. "You're wasted on acoustic. I saw you play before in that terrible band of yours, but you were really good, even for a child such as yourself."

"Thanks. I think."

"You're welcome. I'm not here for flattery. I'm here for recruitment."

"Sorry. I'm a pacifist."

"Funny! I'm a dyke, one who likes to ask and tell, so I'm also ill-suited for the military. No, I'm putting together a band. I think you're an outrageously talented guitar player so I'm here to rob the cradle, artistically speaking."

I was barely sixteen years old and a little bit intimidated by this ballsy chick, but I'd said why not. "Who else is in the band?"

"Me on drums. You on guitar."

"And?"

"Those are the most important parts, don't you think? Fantastic drummers and singing guitar players don't grow on trees, not even in Oregon. Don't worry, I'll fill in the blanks. I'm Liz by the way." She stuck out her hand. It was crusted with calluses, always a good sign on a drummer.

Within a month, Liz had drafted Fitzy and Mike, and we'd christened ourselves Shooting Star and started writing songs together. A month after that, we had our first gig. It was another house party, but nothing like the ones I'd played with Infinity 89. Right from the get-go, something was different. When I slashed out my first chord, it was like turning off a light. Everything just fell silent. We had people's attention and we kept it. In the empty space between songs, people cheered and then got quiet, anticipating our next song. Over time, they'd start shouting requests. After a while, they got to know our lyrics so well that they'd sing along, which was handy when I spaced a lyric.

Pretty soon, we moved on to playing in bigger clubs. I could sometimes make out bar sounds in the background—the clink of glasses, the shouts of orders to a bartender. I also started to hear people scream my name for the first time. "Adam!" "Over here!" A lot of those voices belonged to girls.

The girls I mostly ignored. At this point, I'd started obsessing about a girl who never came to our shows but who I'd seen playing cello at school. And when Mia had become my girlfriend, and then started coming to my shows—and to my surprise, seemed to actually enjoy, if not the gigs, then at least our music—I sometimes listened for her. I wanted to hear her voice calling out my name, even though I knew that was something she'd never do. She was a reluctant plus-one. She tended to hang backstage and watch me with a solemn intensity. Even when she loosened up enough to sometimes watch the show like a normal person, from the audience, she remained pretty reserved. But still, I listened for the sound of her voice. It never seemed to matter that I didn't hear it. Listening for her was half the fun.

As the band got bigger and the shows got bigger, the cheers just grew louder. And then for a while, it all went quiet. There was no music. No band. No fans. No Mia.

When it came back—the music, the gigs, the crowds—it all sounded different. Even during that two-week tour right on the heels of *Collateral Damage*'s release, I could tell how much had changed just by how different everything sounded. The wall of sound as we played enveloped the band, almost as if we were playing in a bubble made of nothing other than our own noise. And in between the songs, there was this screaming and shrieking. Soon, much sooner than I ever could've imagined, we were playing these enormous venues: arenas and stadiums, to more than fifteen thousand fans.

At these venues, there are just so many people, and so much sound, that it's almost impossible to differentiate a specific voice. All I hear, aside from our own instruments now blaring out of the most powerful speakers available, is that wild scream from the crowd when we're backstage and the lights go down right before we go out. And once we're onstage, the constant shrieking of the crowd melds so it sounds like the furious howl of a hurricane; some nights I swear I can feel the breath of those fifteen thousand screams.

I don't like this sound. I find the monolithic nature of it disorienting. For a few gigs, we traded our wedge monitors for in-ear pieces. It was perfect sound, as though we were in the studio, the roar of the crowd blocked off. But that was even worse in a way. I feel so disconnected from the crowds as it is, by the distance between them and us, a distance separated by a vast expanse of stage and an army of security keeping fans from bounding up to touch us or stage-dive the way they used to. But more than that, I don't like that it's so hard to hear any one single voice break through. I dunno. Maybe I'm still listening for that one voice.

Every so often during a show, though, as me or Mike pause to retune our guitars or someone takes a swig from a bottle of water, I'll pause and strain to pick out a voice from the crowd. And every so often, I can. Can hear someone shouting for a specific song or screaming *I love you!* Or chanting my name.

～

As I stand here on the Brooklyn Bridge I'm thinking about those stadium shows, of their hurricane wail of white noise. Because all I can hear now is a roaring in my head, a wordless howl as Mia disappears and I try to let her.

But there's something else, too. A small voice trying to break through, to puncture the roar of nothingness. And the voice grows stronger and stronger, and it's *my* voice this time and it's asking a question: *How does she know?*

EIGHTEEN

Are you happy in your misery?
Resting peaceful in desolation?
It's the final tie that binds us
The sole source of my consolation

"BLUE"

COLLATERAL DAMAGE, TRACK 6

Mia's gone.

The bridge looks like a ghost ship from another time even as it fills up with the most twenty-first-century kind of people, early-morning joggers.

And me, alone again.

But I'm still standing. I'm still breathing. And somehow, I'm okay.

But still the question is gaining momentum and volume: *How does she know?* Because I never told anyone what I asked of her. Not the nurses. Not the grandparents. Not Kim. And not Mia. So how does she know?

If you stay, I'll do whatever you want. I'll quit the band, go with you to New York. But if you need me to go away, I'll do that, too. Maybe coming back to your old life would just be too painful, maybe it'd be easier for you to erase us. And that would suck, but I'd do it. I can lose you like that if I don't lose you today. I'll let you go. If you stay.

That was my vow. And it's been my secret. My burden. My shame. That I asked her to stay. That she listened. Because after I promised her what I promised her, and played her a Yo-Yo Ma cello piece, it had seemed as if she *had* heard. She'd squeezed my hand and I'd thought it was going to be like in the movies, but all she'd done was squeeze. And stayed unconscious. But that squeeze had turned out to be her first voluntary muscle movement; it was followed by more squeezes, then by her eyes opening for a flutter or two, and then longer. One of the nurses had explained that Mia's brain was like a baby bird, trying to poke its way out of an eggshell, and that squeeze was the beginning of an emergence that went on for a few days until she woke up and asked for water.

Whenever she talked about the accident, Mia said the entire week was a blur. She didn't remember a thing. And I wasn't about to tell her about the promise I'd made. A promise that in the end, I was forced to keep.

But *she knew.*

No wonder she hates me.

In a weird way, it's a relief. I'm so tired of carrying this secret around. I'm so tired of feeling bad for making her live and feeling angry at her for living without me and feeling like a hypocrite for the whole mess.

I stand there on the bridge for a while, letting her get away, and then I walk the remaining few hundred feet to the ramp down. I've seen dozens of taxis pass by on the roadway below, so even though I have no clue where I am, I'm pretty sure I'll find a cab to bring me back to my hotel. But when I get down the ramp, I'm in a plaza area, not where the car traffic lets out. I flag down a jogger, a middle-aged guy chugging off the bridge, and ask where I can get a taxi, and he points me toward a bunch of buildings. "There's usually a queue on week-days. I don't know about weekends, but I'm sure you'll find a cab somewhere."

He's wearing an iPod and has pulled out the earbuds to talk to me, but the music is still playing. And it's Fugazi. The guy is running to Fugazi, the very tail end of "Smallpox Champion." Then the song clicks over and it's "Wild Horses" by the Rolling Stones. And the music, it's like, I dunno, fresh bread on an empty stom-ach or a woodstove on a frigid day. It's reaching out of the earbuds and beckoning me.

The guy keeps looking at me. "Are you Adam Wilde?

From Shooting Star?" he asks. Not at all fanlike, just curious.

It takes a lot of effort to stop listening to the music and give him my attention. "Yeah." I reach out my hand.

"I don't mean to be rude," he says after we shake, "but what are you doing walking around Brooklyn at six thirty on a Saturday morning? Are you lost or something?"

"No, I'm not lost. Not anymore anyway."

Mick Jagger is crooning away and I practically have to bite my lip to keep from singing along. It used to be I never went anywhere without my tunes. And then it was like everything else, take it or leave it. But now I'll take it. Now I *need* it. "Can I ask you for an insanely huge and just plain insane favor?" I ask.

"Okaaay?"

"Can I borrow your iPod? Just for the day? If you give me your name and address, I'll have it messengered over to you. I promise you'll have it back by tomorrow's run."

He shakes his head, laughs. "One butt-crack-of-dawn run a weekend is enough for me, but yeah, you can borrow it. The buzzer on my building doesn't work, so just deliver it to Nick at the Southside Café on Sixth Avenue in Brooklyn. I'm in there every morning."

"Nick. Southside Café. Sixth Avenue. Brooklyn. I won't forget. I promise."

"I believe you," he says, spooling the wires. "I'm afraid you won't find any Shooting Star on there."

"Better yet. I'll have this back to you by tonight."

"Don't worry about it," he says. "Battery was fully charged when I left so you should be good for at least . . . an hour. The thing's a dinosaur." He chuckles softly. Then he takes off running, tossing a wave at me without looking back.

I plug myself into the iPod; it's truly battered. I make a note to get him a new one when I return this one. I scroll through his collection—everything from Charlie Parker to Minutemen to Yo La Tengo. He's got all these playlists. I choose one titled Good Songs. And when the piano riff at the start of the New Pornographers' "Challengers" kicks in, I know I've put myself in good hands. Next up is some Andrew Bird, followed by a kick-ass Billy Bragg and Wilco song I haven't heard in years and then Sufjan Stevens's "Chicago," which is a song I used to love but had to stop listening to because it always made me feel too stirred up. But now it's just right. It's like a cool bath after a fever sweat, helping to soothe the itch of all those unanswerable questions I just can't be tormenting myself with anymore.

I spin the volume up all the way, so it's blasting even

my battle-worn eardrums. That, along with the racket of downtown Brooklyn waking up—metal grates grinding and buses chugging—is pretty damn loud. So when a voice pierces the din, I almost don't hear it. But there it is, the voice I've been listening for all these years.

"Adam!" it screams.

I don't believe it at first. I turn off Sufjan. I look around. And then there she is, in front of me now, her face streaked with tears. Saying my name again, like it's the first word I've ever heard.

I let go. I truly did. But there she is. Right in front of me.

"I thought I'd lost you. I went back and looked for you on the bridge but I didn't see you and I figured you'd walked back to the Manhattan side and I got this dumb idea that I could beat you over in a cab and ambush you on the other side. I know this is selfish. I heard what you said up there on the bridge, but we can't leave it like that. *I* can't. Not again. We have to say good-bye differently. Bet—"

"Mia?" I interrupt. My voice is a question mark and a caress. It stops her babbling cold. "How did you know?"

The question is out of the blue. Yet she seems to know exactly what I'm asking about. "Oh. That," she says. "That's complicated."

I start to back away from her. I have no right to ask

her, and she isn't under any obligation to tell me. "It's okay. We're good now. *I'm* good now."

"No, Adam, stop," Mia says.

I stop.

"I want to tell you. I *need* to tell you everything. I just think I need some coffee before I can get it together enough to explain."

She leads me out of downtown into a historic district to a bakery on a cobblestoned street. Its windows are darkened, the door locked, by all signs the place is closed. But Mia knocks and within a minute a bushy-haired man with flour clinging to his unruly beard swings open the door and shouts *bonjour* to Mia and kisses her on both cheeks. Mia introduces me to Hassan, who disappears into the bakery, leaving the door open so that the warm aroma of butter and vanilla waft into the morning air. He returns with two large cups of coffee and a brown paper bag, already staining dark with butter. She hands me my coffee, and I open it to see it's steaming and black just like I like it.

It's morning now. We find a bench on the Brooklyn Heights Promenade, another one of Mia's favorite New York spots, she tells me. It's right on the East River, with Manhattan so close you can almost touch it. We sit in companionable silence, sipping our coffee, eating Hassan's still-warm croissants. And it feels so good, so like old times that part of me would like to just click a magic stopwatch, exist in this moment forever. Except there are no magic stopwatches and there are questions that need to be answered. Mia, however, seems in no rush. She sips, she chews, she looks out at the city. Finally, when she's drained her coffee, she turns to me.

"I didn't lie before when I said I didn't remember anything about the accident or after," she begins. "But then I did start remembering things. Not exactly remembering, but hearing details of things and having them feel intensely familiar. I told myself it was because I'd heard the stories over and over, but that wasn't it.

"Fast-forward about a year and a half. I'm on my seventh or eighth therapist."

"So you *are* in therapy?"

She gives me a cockeyed look. "Of course I am. I used to go through shrinks like shoes. They all told me the same thing."

"Which is?"

"That I was *angry*. That I was *angry* the accident happened. That I was *angry* I was the only survivor. That I was *angry* at you." She turns to me with an apologetic grimace. "The other stuff all made sense, but *you* I didn't get. I mean, why you? But I was. I could feel how . . ." she trails off for a second, "furious I was," she finishes quietly. "There were all the obvious rea-

sons, how you withdrew from me, how much the accident changed us. But it didn't add up to this *lethal* fury I
suddenly felt once I got away. I think really, somewhere
in me, I must've known all along that you asked me to
stay—way before I actually remembered it. Does that
make *any* sense?"

No. Yes. I don't know. "None of this makes *sense*,"
I say.

"I know. So, I was angry with you. I didn't know
why. I was angry with the world. I did know why. I
hated all my therapists for being useless. I was this little ball of self-destructive fury, and none of them could
do anything but tell me that I was a little ball of self-
destructive fury. Until I found Nancy, not one of them
helped me as much as my Juilliard profs did. I mean,
hello! I *knew* I was angry. Tell me what to *do* with the
anger, please. Anyhow, Ernesto suggested hypnotherapy.
It helped him quit smoking, I guess." She elbows me in
the ribs.

Of course Mr. Perfect wouldn't smoke. And of
course, he'd be the one who helped Mia unearth the
reason she hates me.

"It was kind of risky," Mia continues. "Hypno-
sis tends to unlock hidden memories. Some trauma is
just too much for the conscious mind to handle and
you have to go in through a back door to access it. So I

reluctantly submitted to a few sessions. It wasn't what I thought it would be. No swinging amulet, no metronome. It was more like those guided imagery exercises they'd sometimes have us do at camp. At first, nothing happened, and then I went to Vermont for the summer and quit.

"But a few weeks later, I started to get these flashes. Random flashes. Like I could remember a surgery, could actually hear the specific music the doctors played in the operating room. I thought about calling them to ask if what I remembered was true, but so much time had passed I doubted they'd remember. Besides, I didn't really feel like I needed to ask them. My dad used to say that when I was born I looked so totally familiar to him, he was overwhelmed with this feeling that he'd known me all his life, which was funny, considering how little I looked like him or Mom. But when I had my first memories, I felt that same certainty, that they were real and mine. I didn't put the pieces together fully until I was working on a cello piece—a lot of memories seem to hit when I'm playing—anyhow, it was Gershwin, *Andante con moto e poco rubato*."

I open my mouth to say something, but at first nothing comes out. "I played you that," I finally say.

"I know." She doesn't seem surprised by my confirmation.

I lean forward, put my head between my knees, and take deep breaths. I feel Mia's hand gently touch the back of my neck.

"Adam?" Her voice is tentative. "There's more. And here's where it gets a little freaky. It makes a certain sense to me that my mind somehow recorded the things that were happening around my body while I was unconscious. But there are other things, other memories. . . ."

"Like what?" My voice is a whisper.

"Most of it is hazy, but I have certain strong memories of things I couldn't know because I wasn't there. I have this one memory. It's of you. It's dark out. And you're standing outside the hospital entrance under the floodlights, waiting to come see me. You're wearing your leather jacket, and looking up. Like you're looking for me. Did you do that?"

Mia cups my chin up and lifts my face, this time apparently seeking some affirmation that this moment was real. I want to tell her that she's right, but I've completely lost the ability to speak. My expression, however, seems to offer the validation she's after. She nods her head slightly. "How? How, Adam? How could I know that?"

I'm not sure if the question's rhetorical or if she thinks I have a clue to her metaphysical mystery. And I'm in no state to answer either way because I'm crying. I don't realize it till I taste the salt against my lips. I can't remember the last time I've cried but, once I accept the mortification of sniveling like a baby, the floodgates open and I'm sobbing now, in front of Mia. In front of the whole damn world.

NINETEEN

The first time I ever saw Mia Hall was six years ago. Our high school had this arts program and if you chose music as your elective, you could take music classes or opt for independent study to practice in the studios. Mia and I both went for the independent study.

I'd seen her playing her cello a couple of times but nothing had really registered. I mean she was cute and all, but, not exactly my type. She was a classical musician. I was a rock guy. Oil and water and all that.

I didn't really notice her until the day I saw her *not* playing. She was just sitting in one of the soundproof practice booths, her cello resting gently against her knees, her bow poised a few inches above the bridge. Her eyes were closed and her brow was a little furrowed. She was so still, it seemed like she'd taken a brief vacation from her body. And even though she wasn't moving, even though her eyes were closed, I somehow knew that she was listening to music then, was grabbing the notes from the silence, like a squirrel gathering acorns for the winter, before she got down to the business of playing. I stood there, suddenly riveted by her, until she seemed to wake up and start playing with this intense concentration. When she finally looked at me, I hustled away.

After that, I became kind of fascinated by her and by what I guessed was her ability to hear music in the silence. Back then, I'd wanted to be able to do that, too. So I took to watching her play, and though I told myself the reason for my attention was because she was as dedicated a musician as I was and that she was cute, the truth was that I also wanted to understand what she heard in the silence.

During all the time we were together, I don't think I ever found out. But once I was with her, I didn't need to. We were both music-obsessed, each in our own way. If we didn't entirely understand the other person's obsession, it didn't matter, because we understood our own.

I know the exact moment Mia is talking about. Kim and I had driven to the hospital in Sarah's pink Dodge Dart. I don't remember asking Liz's girlfriend to borrow her car. I don't remember driving it. I don't remember piloting the car up into the hills where the hospital is or how I even knew the way. Just that one minute I was in a theater in downtown Portland, sound-checking for that night's show when Kim showed up to deliver the awful news. And the next minute I was standing outside the hospital.

What Mia inexplicably remembers, it's sort of the first pinpoint of clarity in that whole petri-dish blur between hearing the news and arriving at the trauma center. Kim and I had just parked the car and I'd walked out of the garage ahead of her. I'd needed a couple of seconds to gather my strength, to steel myself for what I was about to face. And I'd remembered looking at the hulking hospital building and wondering if Mia was somewhere in there, and feeling a heart-in-throat panic that she'd died in the time it had taken Kim to fetch me. But then I'd felt this wave of something, not really hope, not really relief, but just a sort of knowledge that Mia was still in there. And that had been enough to pull me through the doors.

They say that things happen for a reason, but I don't know that I buy that. I don't know that I'll ever see a reason for what happened to Kat, Denny, and Teddy that day. But it took forever to get in to see Mia. I got turned away from the ICU by Mia's nurses, and then Kim and I devised this whole plan to sneak in. I don't think I realized it at the time, but I think in a weird way, I was probably stalling. I was gathering my strength. I didn't want to lose it in front of her. I guess part of me somehow knew that Mia, deep in her coma, would be able to tell.

Of course, I ended up losing it in front of her anyway. When I finally saw her the first time, I almost blew chunks. Her skin looked like tissue paper. Her eyes were covered with tape. Tubes ran in and out of every part of her body, pumping liquids and blood in and draining some scary-ass shit out. I'm ashamed to say it, but when I first came in, I wanted to run away.

But I couldn't. I wouldn't. So instead, I just focused on the part of her that still looked remotely like Mia—her hands. There were monitors stuck to her fingers, but they still looked like her hands. I touched the fingertips of her left hand, which felt worn and smooth, like old leather. I ran my fingers across the nubby calluses of her thumbs. Her hands were freezing, just like they always were, so I warmed them, just like I always did.

And it was while warming her hands that I thought about how lucky it was that they looked okay. Because without hands, there'd be no music and without music, she'd have lost everything. And I remember thinking that somehow Mia had to realize that, too. That she needed to be reminded that she had the music to come back to. I ran out of the ICU, part of me fearing that I might never see her alive again, but somehow knowing that I had to do this one thing. When I came back, I played her the Yo-Yo Ma.

And that's also when I made her the promise. The promise that she's held me to.

I did the right thing. I know it now. I must've always known, but it's been so hard to see through all my anger. And it's okay if she's angry. It's even okay if she hates me. It was selfish what I asked her to do, even if it wound up being the most unselfish thing I've ever done. The most unselfish thing I'll have to *keep* doing.

But I'd do it again. I know that now. I'd make that promise a thousand times over and lose her a thousand times over to have heard her play last night or to see her in the morning sunlight. Or even without that. Just to know that she's somewhere out there. Alive.

Mia watches me lose my shit all over the Promenade. She bears witness as the fissures open up, the lava leaking out, this great explosion of what, I guess to her, must look like grief.

But I'm not crying out of grief. I'm crying out of gratitude.

TWENTY

Someone wake me when it's over
When the evening silence softens golden
Just lay me on a bed of clover
Oh, I need help with this burden

"HUSH"
COLLATERAL DAMAGE, TRACK 13

When I get a grip over myself and calm down, my limbs feel like they're made of dead wood. My eyes start to droop. I just drank a huge cup of insanely strong coffee, and it might as well have been laced with sleeping pills. I could lie down right here on this bench. I turn to Mia. I tell her I need to sleep

"My place is a few blocks away," she says. "You can crash there."

I have that floppy calm that follows a cry. I haven't felt this way since I was a child, a sensitive kid, who would scream at some injustice or another until, all

cried out, my mother would tuck me into bed. I picture Mia, tucking me into a single boy's bed, pulling the
Buzz Lightyear sheets up to my chin.

It's full-on morning now. People are awake and out
and about. As we walk, the quiet residential area gives
way to a commercial strip, full of boutiques, cafés, and
the hipsters who frequent them. I'm recognized. But I
don't bother with any subterfuge—no sunglasses, no cap.
I don't try to hide at all. Mia weaves among the growing crowds and then turns off onto a leafy side street full
of brownstones and brick buildings. She stops in front
of a small redbrick carriage house. "Home sweet home.
It's a sublet from a professional violinist who's with the
Vienna Philharmonic now. I've been here a record nine
months!"

I follow her into the most compact house I've ever
seen. The first floor consists of little more than a living
room and kitchen with a sliding-glass door leading out
to a garden that's twice as deep as the house. There's
a white sectional couch, and she motions for me to lie
down on it. I kick off my shoes and flop onto one of the
sections, sinking into the plush cushions. Mia lifts my
head, places a pillow underneath it, and a soft blanket
over me, tucking me in just as I'd hoped she would.

I listen for the sound of her footsteps on the stairs

up to what must be the bedroom, but instead, I feel a slight bounce in the upholstery as Mia takes up a position on the other end of the couch. She rustles her legs together a few times. Her feet are only inches away from my own. Then she lets out a long sigh and her breathing slows into a rhythmic pattern. She's asleep. Within minutes, so am I.

When I wake up, light is flooding the apartment, and I feel so refreshed that for a second I'm sure I've slept for ten hours and have missed my flight. But a quick glance at the kitchen clock shows me it's just before two o'clock, still Saturday. I've only been asleep for a few hours, and I have to meet Aldous at the airport at five.

Mia's still asleep, breathing deeply and almost snoring. I watch her there for a while. She looks so peaceful and so familiar. Even before I became the insomniac I am now, I always had problems falling asleep at night, whereas Mia would read a book for five minutes, roll onto her side, and be gone. A strand of hair has fallen onto her face and it gets sucked into her mouth and back out again with each inhalation and exhalation. Without even thinking I lean over and move the strand away, my finger accidentally brushing her lips. It feels so natural, so much like the last three years haven't passed, that I'm almost tempted to stroke her cheeks, her chin, her forehead.

Almost. But not quite. It's like I'm seeing Mia through a prism and she's mostly the girl I knew but something has changed, the angles are off, and so now, the idea of me touching a sleeping Mia isn't sweet or romantic. It's stalkerish.

I straighten up and stretch out my limbs. I'm about to wake her—but can't quite bring myself to. Instead, I walk around her house. I was so out of it when we came in a few hours ago, I didn't really take it in. Now that I do, I see that it looks oddly like the house Mia grew up in. There's the same mismatched jumble of pictures on the wall—a Velvet Elvis, a 1955 poster advertising the World Series between the Brooklyn Dodgers and the New York Yankees—and the same decorative touches, like chili-pepper lights festooning the doorways.

And photos, they're everywhere, hanging on the walls, covering every inch of counter and shelf space. Hundreds of photos of her family, including what seem to be the photos that once hung in her old house. There's Kat and Denny's wedding portrait; a shot of Denny in a spiked leather jacket holding a tiny baby Mia in one of his hands; eight-year-old Mia, a giant grin on her face, clutching her cello; Mia and Kat holding a red-faced Teddy, minutes after he was born. There's even that heartbreaking shot of Mia reading to Teddy, the one that I could never bear to look at at Mia's grandparents', though somehow here, in Mia's place, it doesn't give me that same kick in the gut.

I walk through the small kitchen, and there's a veritable gallery of shots of Mia's grandparents in front of a plethora of orchestra pits, of Mia's aunts and uncles and cousins hiking through Oregon mountains or lifting up pints of ale. There are a jumble of shots of Henry and Willow and Trixie and the little boy who must be Theo. There are pictures of Kim and Mia from high school and one of the two of them posing on top of the Empire State Building—a jolting reminder that their relationship wasn't truncated, they have a history of which I know nothing. There's another picture of Kim, wearing a flak jacket, her hair tangled and down and blowing in a dusty wind.

There are pictures of musicians in formal wear, holding flutes of champagne. Of a bright-eyed man in a tux with a mass of wild curls holding a baton, and the same guy conducting a bunch of ratty-looking kids, and then him again, next to a gorgeous black woman, kissing a not-ratty-looking kid. This must be Ernesto.

I wander into the back garden for my wake-up smoke. I pat my pockets, but all I find there is my wallet, my sunglasses, the borrowed iPod, and the usual assortment of guitar picks that always seem to live on me. Then I remember that I must have left my cigarettes on the bridge. No smokes. No pills. I guess today is the banner day for quitting bad habits.

I come back inside and take another look around. This isn't the house I expected. From all her talk of moving, I'd imagined a place full of boxes, something impersonal and antiseptic. And despite what she'd said about spirits, I wouldn't have guessed that she'd surround herself so snugly with her ghosts.

Except for my ghost. There's not a single picture of me, even though Kat included me in so many of the family shots; she'd even hung a framed photo of me and Mia and Teddy in Halloween costumes above their old living-room mantel, a place of honor in the Hall home. But not here. There are none of the silly shots Mia and I used to take of each other and of ourselves, kissing or mugging while one of us held the camera at arm's length. I loved those pictures. They always cut off half a head or were obscured by someone's finger, but they seemed to capture something true.

I'm not offended. Earlier, I might've been. But I get it now. Whatever place I held in Mia's life, in Mia's heart, was irrevocably altered that day in the hospital three and a half years ago.

Closure. I loathe that word. Shrinks love it. Bryn loves it. She says that I've never had *closure* with Mia.

"More than five million people have bought and listened to my closure," is my standard reply.

Standing here, in this quiet house where I can hear the birds chirping out back, I think I'm kind of getting the concept of closure. It's no big dramatic before-after. It's more like that melancholy feeling you get at the end of a really good vacation. Something special is ending, and you're sad, but you can't be that sad because, hey, it was good while it lasted, and there'll be other vacations, other good times. But they won't be with Mia—or with Bryn.

I glance at the clock. I need to get back to Manhattan, pack up my stuff, reply to the most urgent of the emails that have no doubt piled up, and get myself to the airport. I'll need to get a cab out of here, and before that I'll need to wake Mia up and say a proper goodbye.

I decide to make coffee. The smell of it alone used to rouse her. On the mornings I used to sleep at her house, sometimes I woke up early to hang with Teddy. After I let her sleep to a decent hour, I'd take the percolator right into her room and waft it around until she lifted her head from the pillow, her eyes all dreamy and soft.

I go into the kitchen and instinctively seem to know where everything is, as though this is my kitchen and

I've made coffee here a thousand times before. The metal percolator is in the cabinet above the sink. The coffee in a jar on the freezer door. I spoon the rich, dark powder into the chamber atop the percolator, then fill it with water and put it on the stove. The hissing sound fills the air, followed by the rich aroma. I can almost see it, like a cartoon cloud, floating across the room, prodding Mia awake.

And sure enough, before the whole pot is brewed, she's stretching out on the couch, gulping a bit for air like she does when she's waking up. When she sees me in her kitchen, she looks momentarily confused. I can't tell if it's because I'm bustling around like a housewife or just because I'm here in the first place. Then I remember what she said about her daily wake-up call of loss. "Are you remembering it all over again?" I ask the question. Out loud. Because I want to know and because she asked me to ask.

"No," she says. "Not this morning." She yawns, then stretches again. "I thought I dreamed last night. Then I smelled coffee."

"Sorry," I mutter.

She's smiling as she kicks off her blanket. "Do you really think that if you don't mention my family I'll forget them?"

"No," I admit. "I guess not."

"And as you can see, I'm not trying to forget." Mia motions to the photos.

"I was looking at those. Pretty impressive gallery you've got. Of everyone."

"Thanks. They keep me company."

I look at the pictures, imagining that one day Mia's own children will fill more of her frames, creating a new family for her, a continuing generation that I won't be a part of.

"I know they're just pictures," she continues, "but some days they really help me get up in the morning. Well, them, and coffee."

Ahh, the coffee. I go to the kitchen and open the cabinets where I know the cups will be, though I'm a little startled to find that even these are the same collection of 1950s and 60s ceramic mugs that I've used so many times before; amazed that she's hauled them from dorm to dorm, from apartment to apartment. I look around for my favorite mug, the one with the dancing coffeepots on it, and am so damn happy to find it's still here. It's almost like having my picture on the wall, too. A little piece of me still exists, even if the larger part of me can't.

I pour myself a cup, then pour Mia's, adding a dash of half-and-half, like she takes it.

"I like the pictures," I say. "Keeps things interesting."

Mia nods, blows ripples into her coffee.

"And I miss them, too," I say. "Every day."

She looks surprised at that. Not that I miss them, but, I guess by my admitting it, finally. She nods solemnly. "I know," she says.

She walks around the room, running her fingers lightly along the picture frames. "I'm running out of space," she says. "I had to put up a bunch of Kim's recent shots in the bathroom. Have you talked to her lately?"

She must know what I did to Kim. "No."

"Really? Then you don't know about the *scandale*?"

I shake my head.

"She dropped out of college last year. When the war flared up in Afghanistan, Kim decided, screw it, I want to be a photographer and the best education is in the field. So she just took her cameras and off she went. She started selling all these shots to the AP and the *New York Times*. She cruises around in one of those burkas and hides all her photographic equipment underneath the robes and then whips them off to get her shot."

"I'll bet Mrs. Schein loves that." Kim's mom was notoriously overprotective. The last I'd heard of her, she was having a freak-out that Kim was going to school across the country, which, Kim had said, was precisely the point.

Mia laughs. "At first, Kim told her family she was just

taking a semester off, but now she's getting really successful so she's officially dropped out, and Mrs. Schein
has officially had a nervous breakdown. And then there's
the fact that Kim's a nice Jewish girl in a very Mus-
lim country." Mia blows on her coffee and sips. "But,
on the other hand, now Kim gets her stuff in the *New
York Times,* and she just got a feature assignment for
National Geographic, so it gives Mrs. Schein some brag-
ging ammo."

"Hard for a mother to resist," I say.

"She's a big Shooting Star fan, you know?"

"Mrs. Schein? I always had her pegged as more hip-
hop."

Mia grins. "No. She's into death metal. Hard core.
Kim. She saw you guys play in Bangkok. Said it poured
rain and you played right through it."

"She was at that show? I wish she would've come
backstage, said hi," I say, even though I know why she
wouldn't have. Still, she came to the show. She must
have forgiven me a little bit.

"I told her the same thing. But she had to leave
right away. She was supposed to be in Bangkok for some
R & R, but that rain you were playing in was actually
a cyclone somewhere else and she had to run off and
cover it. She's a very badass shutterbabe these days."

I think of Kim chasing Taliban insurgents and ducking flying trees. It's surprisingly easy to imagine. "It's funny," I begin.

"What is?" Mia asks.

"Kim being a war photographer. All Danger Girl."

"Yeah, it's a laugh riot."

"That's not how I meant. It's just: Kim. You. Me. We all came from this nowhere town in Oregon, and look at us. All three of us have gone to, well, extremes. You gotta admit, it's kind of weird."

"It's not weird at all," Mia says, shaking out a bowl of cornflakes. "We were all forged in the crucible. Now come on, have some cereal."

I'm not hungry. I'm not even sure I can eat a single cornflake, but I sit down because my place at the Hall family table has just been restored.

＊

Time has a weight to it, and right now I can feel it heavy over me. It's almost three o'clock. Another day is half over and tonight I leave for the tour. I hear the clicking of the antique clock on Mia's wall. I let the minutes go by longer than I should before I finally speak.

"We both have our flights. I should probably get moving," I say. My voice sounds faraway but I feel weirdly calm. "Are there taxis around here?"

"No, we get back and forth to Manhattan by river raft," she jokes. "You can call a car," she adds after a moment.

I stand up, make my way toward the kitchen counter where Mia's phone sits. "What's the number?" I ask.

"Seven-one-eight," Mia begins. Then she interrupts herself. "Wait."

At first I think she has to pause to recall the number, but I see her eyes, at once unsure and imploring.

"There's one last thing," she continues, her voice hesitant. "Something I have that really belongs to you."

"My Wipers T-shirt?"

She shakes her head. "That's long gone, I'm afraid. Come on. It's upstairs."

I follow her up the creaking steps. At the top of the narrow landing to my right I can see her bedroom with its slanted ceilings. To my left is a closed door. Mia opens it, revealing a small studio. In the corner is a cabinet with a keypad. Mia punches in a code and the door opens.

When I see what she pulls out of the cabinet, at first I'm like, *Oh, right, my guitar.* Because here in Mia's little house in Brooklyn is my old electric guitar, my Les Paul Junior. The guitar I bought at a pawnshop with my pizza-delivery earnings when I was a teenager. It's the guitar I used to record all of our stuff leading up to, and including, *Collateral Damage*. It's the guitar I auctioned off for charity and have regretted doing so ever since.

It's sitting in its old case, with my old Fugazi and K Records stickers, with the stickers from Mia's dad's old band, even. Everything is the same, the strap, the dent from when I'd dropped it off a stage. Even the dust smells familiar.

And I'm just taking it all in, so it's a few seconds before it really hits me. This is *my* guitar. *Mia* has my guitar. Mia is the one who *bought* my guitar for some exorbitant sum, which means that Mia knew it was up for auction. I look around the room. Among the sheet music and cello paraphernalia is a pile of magazines, my face peeking out from the covers. And then I remember something back on the bridge, Mia justifying why she left me by reciting the lyrics to "Roulette."

And suddenly, it's like I've been wearing earplugs all night and they've fallen out, and everything that was muffled is now clear. But also so loud and jarring.

Mia has my guitar. It's such a straightforward thing and yet I don't know that I would've been more surprised had Teddy popped out of the closet. I feel faint. I sit down. Mia stands right in front of me, holding my guitar by the neck, offering it back to me.

"You?" is all I can manage to choke out.

"Always me," she replies softly, bashfully. "Who else?"

My brain has vacated my body. My speech is reduced to the barest of basics. "But . . . why?"

"Somebody had to save it from the Hard Rock Café," Mia says with a laugh. But I can hear the potholes in her voice, too.

"But . . ." I grasp for the words like a drowning man reaching for floating debris," . . . you said you *hated* me?"

Mia lets out a long, deep sigh. "I know. I needed someone to hate, and you're the one I love the most, so it fell to you."

She's holding out the guitar, nudging it toward me. She wants me to take it, but I couldn't lift a cotton ball right now.

She keeps staring, keeps offering.

"But what about Ernesto?"

A look of puzzlement flits across her face, followed by amusement. "He's my mentor, Adam. My friend. He's *married*." She looks down for a beat. When her gaze returns, her amusement has hardened into defensiveness. "Besides, why should you care?"

Go back to your ghost, I hear Bryn telling me. But she has it wrong. *Bryn* is the one who's been living with the ghost—the specter of a man who never stopped loving someone else.

"There never would've been a Bryn if you hadn't decided you needed to hate me," I reply.

Mia takes this one square on the chin. "I don't hate you. I don't think I ever really did. It was just anger. And once I faced it head-on, once I understood it, it dissipated." She looks down, takes a deep breath, and exhales a tornado. "I know I owe you some kind of an apology; I've been trying to get it out all night but it's like those words—apology, sorry—are too measly for what you deserve." She shakes her head. "I know what I did to you was so wrong, but at the time it also felt so necessary to my survival. I don't know if those two things can both be true but that's how it was. If it's any comfort, after a while, when it didn't feel necessary anymore, when it felt hugely wrong, all I was left with was the magnitude of my mistake, of my missing you. And I had to watch you from this distance, watch you achieve your dreams, live what seemed like this perfect life."

"It's *not* perfect," I say.

"I get that *now*, but how was I supposed to know? You were so very, very far from me. And I'd accepted that. Accepted that as my punishment for what I'd done. And then . . ." she trails off.

"What?"

She takes a gulp of air and grimaces. "And then Adam Wilde shows up at Carnegie Hall on the biggest night of my career, and it felt like more than a coincidence. It felt like a gift. From them. For my first recital ever, they gave me a cello. And for this one, they gave me you."

Every hair on my body stands on end, my whole body alert with a chill.

She hastily wipes tears from her eyes with the back of her hand and takes a deep breath. "Here, are you going to take this thing or what? I haven't tuned it for a while."

I used to have dreams like this. Mia back from the not-dead, in front of me, alive to me. But it got so even in the dreams I knew they were unreal and could anticipate the blare of my alarm, so I'm kind of listening now, waiting for the alarm to go off. But it doesn't. And when I close my fingers around the guitar, the wood and strings are solid and root me to the earth. They wake me up. And she's still here.

And she's looking at me, at my guitar, and at her cello and at the clock on the windowsill. And I see what she wants, and it's the same thing I've wanted for years now but I can't believe that after all this time, and now that we're out of time, she's asking for it. But still, I give a little nod. She plugs in the guitar, tosses me the cord, and turns on the amp.

"Can you give me an A?" I ask. Mia plucks her cello's

A string. I tune from that and then I strum an A-minor, and as the chord bounces off the walls, I feel that dash of electricity shimmy up my spine in a way it hasn't done for a long, long time.

I look at Mia. She's sitting across from me, her cello between her legs. Her eyes are closed and I can tell she's doing that thing, listening for something in the silence. Then all at once, Mia seems to have heard what she needs to hear. Her eyes are open and on me again, like they never left. She picks up her bow, gestures toward my guitar with a slight tilt of her head. "Are you ready?" she asks.

There are so many things I'd like to tell her, top among them is that I've always been ready. But instead, I turn up the amp, fish a pick out of my pocket, and just say yes.

TWENTY-ONE

We play for what seems like hours, days, years. Or maybe it's seconds. I can't even tell anymore. We speed up, then slow down, we scream our instruments. We grow serious. We laugh. We grow quiet. Then loud. My heart is pounding, my blood is grooving, my whole body is thrumming as I'm remembering: *Concert* doesn't mean standing up like a target in front of thousands of strangers. It means coming together. It means harmony.

When we finally pause, I'm sweating and Mia's panting hard, like she's just sprinted for miles. We sit there in silence, the sound of our rapid breaths slowing in tandem, the beats of our hearts steadying. I look at the clock. It's past five. Mia follows my gaze. She lays down her bow.

"What now?" she asks.

"Schubert? Ramones?" I say, though I know she's not taking requests. But all I can think to do is keep playing because for the first time in a long time there's nothing more I want to do. And I'm scared of what happens when the music ends.

Mia gestures to the digital clock flashing ominously from the windowsill. "I don't think you'll make your flight."

I shrug. Never mind the fact that there are at least ten other flights to London tonight alone. "Can you make yours?"

"I don't *want* to make mine," she says shyly. "I have a spare day before the recitals begin. I can leave tomorrow."

All of a sudden, I picture Aldous pacing in Virgin's departure lounge, wondering where the hell I am, calling a cell phone that's still sitting on some hotel nightstand. I think of Bryn, out in L.A., unaware of an earthquake going down here in New York that's sending a tsunami her way. And I realize that before there's a next, there's a now that needs attending to. "I need to make some phone calls," I tell Mia. "To my manager, who's waiting for me . . . and to Bryn."

"Oh, right, of course," she says, her face falling as she rushes to stand up, almost toppling her cello in her fluster. "The phone's downstairs. And I should call Tokyo, except I'm pretty sure it's the middle of the night, so I'll just email and call later. And my travel agent—"

"Mia," I interrupt.

"What?"

"We'll figure this out."

"Really?" She doesn't look so sure.

I nod, though my own heart is pounding and the puzzle pieces are whirling as Mia places the cordless phone in my hand. I go into her garden where it's private and peaceful in the afternoon light, the summer cicadas chirping up a storm. Aldous picks up on the first ring and the minute I hear his voice and start talking, reassuring him that I'm okay, the plans start coming out of my mouth as though long, long contemplated. I explain that I'm not coming to London now, that I'm not making any music video, or doing any interviews, but that I'll be in England for the kickoff of our European tour and that I'll play every single one of those shows. The rest of the plan that's formulating in my head—part of which already solidified in some nebulous way last night on the bridge—I keep to myself, but I think Aldous senses it.

I can't see Aldous so I can't know if he blinks or flinches or looks surprised, but he doesn't miss a beat. "You'll honor all your tour commitments?" he repeats.

"Yep."

"What am I supposed to say to the band?"

"They can make the video without me if they want. I'll see them at the Guildford Festival," I say referring to the big music festival in England that we're headlining to kick off our tour. "And I'll explain everything then."

"Where you gonna be in the meantime? If anyone needs you."

"Tell anyone not to need me," I answer.

The next call is harder. I wish I hadn't chosen today to give up smoking. Instead, I do the deep breathing exercises like the doctors showed me and just dial. A journey of a thousand miles starts with ten digits, right?

"I thought that might be you," Bryn says when she hears my voice. "Did you lose your phone again? Where are you?"

"I'm in New York still. In Brooklyn." I pause, "With Mia."

Stone silence fills the line and I fill that silence with a monologue that's what? . . . I don't know: a running explanation of the night that happened by accident, an acknowledgment that things never were right between us, right the way she wanted them to be, and as a result, I've been a dick of a boyfriend. I tell her I hope she'll do better with the next guy.

"Yeah, I wouldn't worry about that," she says with an attempt at a cackle, but it doesn't quite come out that way. There's a long pause. I'm waiting for her tirade, her recriminations, all the things I have coming. But she doesn't say anything.

"Are you still there?" I ask.

"Yeah, I'm thinking."

"About what?"

"I'm thinking about whether I'd rather she'd have died."

"Jesus, Bryn!"

"Oh, shut up! You don't get to be the outraged one. Not right now. And the answer's no. I don't wish her dead." She pauses. "Not so sure about you, though." Then she hangs up.

I stand there, still clutching the phone to my ear, taking in Bryn's last words, wondering if there might've been a shred of absolution in her hostility. I don't know if it matters because as I smell the cooling air, I feel release and relief wash over me.

After a while, I look up. Mia's standing at the sliding-glass door, awaiting the all clear. I give her a dazed wave and she slowly makes her way to the bricked patio where I'm standing, still holding the phone. She grabs hold of the top of the phone, like it's a relay baton, about to be passed off. "Is everything okay?" she asks.

"I'm freed, shall we say, from my previous commitments."

"Of the tour?" She sounds surprised.

I shake my head. "Not the tour. But all the crap leading up to it. And my other, um, entanglements."

"Oh."

We both just stand there for a while, grinning like goofballs, still grasping the cordless. Finally, I let it go and then gently detach the receiver from her grasp and place it on the iron table, never releasing my grip of her hand.

I run my thumb over the calluses on her thumb and up and down the bony ridge of her knuckles and wrist. It's at once so natural and such a privilege. This is *Mia* I'm touching. And she's *allowing* it. Not just allowing it, but closing her eyes and leaning into it.

"Is this real. Am I allowed to hold this hand?" I ask, bringing it up to my stubbly cheek.

Mia's smile is melting chocolate. It's a kick-ass guitar solo. It's everything good in this world. *"Mmmm,"* she answers.

I pull her to me. A thousand suns rise from my chest. "Am I allowed to do *this*?" I ask, taking both of her arms in mine and slow-dancing her around the yard.

Her entire face is smiling now. "You're allowed," she murmurs.

I run my hands up and down her bare arms. I spin her around the planters, bursting with fragrant flowers. I bury my head into her hair and breathe the smell of her, of the New York City night that's seared into her. I follow her gaze upward, to the heavens.

"So, do you think they're watching us?" I ask as I give the scar on her shoulder the slightest of kisses and feel arrows of heat shoot through every part of me.

"Who?" Mia asks, leaning into me, shivering slightly.

"Your family. You seem to think they keep tabs on you. You think they can see this?" I loop my arms around her waist and kiss her right behind her ear, the way that used to drive her crazy, the way that, judging by the sharp intake of breath and the nails that dig into my side, still does. It occurs to me that there's seemingly something creepy in my line of questioning, but it doesn't feel that way. Last night, the thought of her family knowing my actions shamed me, but now, it's not like I want them to see *this*, but I want them to *know* about it, about us.

"I like to think they'd give me some privacy," she

says, opening up like a sunflower to the kisses I'm planting on her jaw. "But my neighbors can definitely see this." She runs her hand through my hair and it's like she electrocuted my scalp—if electrocution felt so good.

"Howdy, neighbor," I say, tracing lazy circles around the base of her clavicle with my finger.

Her hands dip under my T-shirt, my dirty, stinky, thank-you lucky black T-shirt. Her touch isn't so gentle anymore. It's probing, the fingertips starting to tap out a Morse code of urgency. "If this goes on much longer, my neighbors are going to get a show," she whispers.

"We are performers, after all," I reply, slipping my hands under her shirt and running them up the length of her long torso then back down again. Our skins reach outward, like magnets, long deprived of their opposite charge.

I run my finger along her neck, her jawline, and then cup her chin in my hand. And stop. We stand there for a moment, staring at each other, savoring it. And then all at once, we slam together. Mia's legs are off the ground, wrapped around my waist, her hands digging in my hair, my hands tangled in hers. And our lips. There isn't enough skin, enough spit, enough time, for the lost years that our lips are trying to make up for as they find each other. We kiss. The electric current switches to high. The lights throughout all of Brooklyn must be surging.

"Inside!" Mia half orders, half begs, and with her legs still wrapped around me, I carry her back into her tiny home, back to the couch where only hours before we'd slept, separately together.

This time we're wide awake. And all together.

⟋

We fall asleep, waking in the middle of the night, ravenous. We order takeout. Eat it upstairs in her bed. It's all like a dream, only the most incredible part is waking up at dawn. With Mia. I see her sleeping form there and feel as happy as I've ever been. I pull her to me and fall back asleep.

But when I wake again a few hours later, Mia's sitting on a chair under the window, her legs wrapped in a tight ball, her body covered in an old afghan that her gran crocheted. And she looks miserable, and the fear that lands like a grenade in my gut is almost as bad as anything I've ever feared with her. And that's saying a lot. All I can think is: *I can't lose you again. It really will kill me this time.*

"What's wrong?" I ask, before I lose the nerve to ask it and do something dumb like walk away before my heart gets truly incinerated.

"I was just thinking about high school," Mia says sadly.

"That would put anyone in a foul mood."

Mia doesn't take the bait. She doesn't laugh. She slumps in the chair. "I was thinking about how we're in the same boat all over again. When I was on my way to Juilliard and you were on your way to, well, where you are now." She looks down, twists the yarn from the blanket around her finger until the skin at the tip goes white. "Except we had more time back then to worry about it. And now we have a day, or had a day. Last night was amazing but it was just one night. I really do have to leave for Japan in like seven hours. And you have the band. Your tour." She presses against her eyes with the heels of her hands.

"Mia, stop!" My voice bounces off her bedroom walls. "We are *not* in high school anymore!"

She looks at me, a question hanging in the air.

"Look, my tour doesn't start for another week."

A feather of hope starts to float across the space between us.

"And you know, I was thinking I was craving some sushi."

Her smile is sad and rueful, not exactly what I was going for. "You'd come to Japan with me?" she asks.

"I'm already there."

"I would love that. But then what—I mean I know

we can figure something out, but I'm going to be on the road so much and . . . ?"

How can it be so unclear to her when it's like the fingers on my hand to me? "I'll be your plus-one," I tell her. "Your groupie. Your roadie. Your whatever. Wherever you go, I go. If you want that. If you don't, I understand."

"No, I want that. Trust me, I want it. But how would that work? With your schedule? With the band?"

I pause. Saying it out loud will finally make it true. "There is no more band. For me, at least, I'm done. After this tour, I'm finished."

"No!" Mia shakes her head with such force, the long strands of her hair thwack the wall behind her. The determined look on her face is one I recognize all too well, and I feel my stomach bottom out. "You can't do that for me," she adds, her voice softening. "I won't take any more free passes."

"Free passes?"

"For the last three years, everyone, except maybe the Juilliard faculty, has given me a free pass. Worse yet, I gave myself a free pass, and that didn't help me at all. I don't want to be that person, who just takes things. I've taken enough from you. I won't let you throw away the thing you love so much to be my caretaker or porter."

"That's just it," I murmur. "I've sort of fallen out of love with music."

"Because of me," Mia says mournfully.

"Because of life," I reply. "I'll always play music. I may even record again, but right now I just need some blank time with my guitar to remember why I got into music in the first place. I'm leaving the band whether you're part of the equation or not. And as for caretaking, if anything, *I'm* the one who needs it. *I'm* the one with the baggage."

I try to make it sound like a joke, but Mia always could see right through my bullshit; the last twenty-four hours have proven that.

She looks at me with those laser beam eyes of hers. "You know, I thought about that a lot these last couple of years," she says in a choked voice. "About who was there for *you*. Who held your hand while you grieved for all that *you'd* lost?"

Mia's words rattle something loose in me and suddenly there are tears all over my damn face again. I haven't cried in three years and now this is like the second time in as many days.

"*It's my turn to see you through,*" she whispers, coming back to me and wrapping me in her blanket as I lose my shit all over again. She holds me until I recover my Y chromosome. Then she turns to me, a slightly faraway look in her eyes. "Your festival's next Saturday, right?" she asks.

I nod.

"I have the two recitals in Japan and one in Korea on Thursday, so I could be out of there by Friday, and you gain a day back when you travel west. And I don't have to be at my next engagement in Chicago for another week after that. So if we flew directly from Seoul to London."

"What are you saying?"

She looks so shy when she asks it, as if there's a snow-ball's chance in hell that I'd ever say no, as if this isn't what I've always wanted.

"Can I come to the festival with you?"

TWENTY-TWO

"How come I never get to go to any concerts?" Teddy asked.

We were all sitting around the table, Mia, Kat, Denny, Teddy, and me, the third child, who'd taken to eating over. You couldn't blame me. Denny was a way better cook than my mom.

"What's that, Little Man?" Denny asked, spooning a portion of mashed potatoes onto Teddy's plate next to the grilled salmon and the spinach that Teddy had tried—unsuccessfully—to refuse.

"I was looking at the old photo albums. And Mia got

to go to all these concerts all the time. When she was a baby, even. And I never even got to go to one. And I'm practically eight."

"You just turned seven five months ago." Kat guffawed.

"Still. Mia went before she could walk. It's not fair!"

"And who ever told you that life was fair?" Kat asked, raising an eyebrow. "Certainly not me. I am a follower of the School of Hard Knocks."

Teddy turned toward an easier target. "Dad?"

"Mia went to concerts because they were my shows, Teddy. It was our family time."

"And you *do* go to concerts," Mia said. "You come to my recitals."

Teddy looked as disgusted as he had when Denny had served him the spinach. "That doesn't count. I want to go to loud concerts and wear the Mufflers." The Mufflers were the giant headphones Mia had worn as a little kid when she'd been taken to Denny's old band's shows. He'd been in a punk band, a very loud punk band.

"The Mufflers have been retired, I'm afraid," Denny said. Mia's dad had long since quit his band. He now was a middle-school teacher who wore vintage suits and smoked pipes.

"You could come to one of my shows," I said, forking a piece of salmon.

Everyone at the table stopped eating and looked at me, the adult members of the Hall family each giving me a different disapproving look. Denny just looked tired at the can of worms I'd opened. Kat looked annoyed for the subversion of her parental authority. And Mia—who, for whatever reason, had this giant church-state wall between her family and my band—was shooting daggers. Only Teddy—up on his knees in his chair, clapping—was still on my team.

"Teddy can't stay up that late," Kat said.

"You let Mia stay up that late when she was little," Teddy shot back.

"*We* can't stay up that late," Denny said wearily.

"And I don't think it's appropriate," Mia huffed.

Immediately, I felt the familiar annoyance in my gut. Because this was the thing I never understood. On one hand, music was this common bond between Mia and me, and me being an all-rock guy *had* to be part of her attraction. And we both knew that the common ground we'd found at her family's house—where we hung out all the time—made it like a haven for us. But she'd all but banned her family from my shows. In the year we'd been together, they'd never been. Even though Denny and Kat had hinted that they'd like to come, Mia was always making up excuses why this show or that was not the right time.

"Appropriate? Did you just say that it's not 'appropriate' for Teddy to come to my show?" I asked, trying to keep my voice level.

"Yes, I did." She couldn't have sounded more defensive or snippy if she'd tried.

Kat and Denny flashed each other a look. Whatever annoyance they'd had with me had turned to sympathy. They knew what Mia's disapproval felt like.

"Okay, first off, you're sixteen. You're not a librarian. So you're not allowed to say 'appropriate.' And second of all, why the hell isn't it?"

"All right, Teddy," Kat said, scooping up Teddy's dinner plate. "You can eat in the living room in front of the TV."

"No way, I want to watch this!"

"SpongeBob?" Denny offered, pulling him by the elbow.

"By the way," I said to Denny and Kat, "the show I was thinking of is this big festival coming up on the coast next month. It'll be during the day, on a weekend, and outside, so not as loud. That's why I thought it'd be cool for Teddy. For all of you, actually."

Kat's expression softened. She nodded. "That does sound fun." Then she gestured to Mia as if to say: *But you've got bigger fish to fry.*

The three of them shuffled out of the kitchen. Mia

was slunk all the way down in her chair, looking both guilty and like there was no way in hell she was going to give an inch.

"What's your problem?" I demanded. "What's your hang-up with your family and my band? Do you think we suck so badly?"

"No, of course not!"

"Do you resent me and your dad talking music all the time?"

"No, I don't mind the rock-talk."

"So, what is it, Mia?"

The tiniest rebel teardrops formed in the edges of her eyes and she angrily swatted them away.

"What? What *is* the matter?" I asked, softening. Mia wasn't prone to crocodile tears, or to any tears, really.

She shook her head. Lips sealed shut.

"Will you just tell me? It can't be worse than what I'm thinking, which is that you're ashamed of Shooting Star because you think we reek to holy hell."

She shook her head again. "You know that's not true. It's just," she paused, as if weighing some big decision. Then she sighed. "The band. When you're with the band, I already have to share you with everyone. I don't want to add my family to that pot, too." Then she lost the battle and started to cry.

All my annoyance melted. "You dumb-ass," I crooned,

kissing her on the forehead. "You don't share me. You own me."

⌒

Mia relented. Her whole family came to the festival. It was a fantastic weekend, twenty Northwest bands, not a rain cloud in sight. The whole thing went down in infamy, spawning a live recorded CD and a series of festivals that continue to this day.

Teddy had insisted on wearing the Mufflers, so Kat had spent an hour grumbling and digging through boxes in the basement until she'd found them.

Mia generally liked to hang backstage at shows but when Shooting Star played, she was right in front of the stage, just clear of the mosh pit, dancing with Teddy the whole time.

TWENTY-THREE

First you inspect me
Then you dissect me
Then you reject me
I wait for the day
That you'll resurrect me

"ANIMATE"
COLLATERAL DAMAGE, TRACK 1

When our flight lands in London, it's pissing down rain, so it feels like home to both of us. It's five in the afternoon when we get in. We're due in Guildford that evening. We play the next night. Then it's countdown till total freedom. Mia and I have worked out a schedule for the next three months while I'm touring and she's touring, breaks here and there where we can overlap, visit, see each other. It's not going to be delightful, but compared to the last three years, it'll still feel like heaven.

It's past eight when we get to the hotel. I've asked Aldous to book me at the same place as the rest of the band, not just for the festival but the duration of the tour. Whatever their feelings are going to be about my leaving Shooting Star, sleeping two miles away ain't gonna minimize them. I haven't mentioned Mia to Aldous or anyone, and miraculously, we've managed to keep her name out of the tabloids so far. No one seems to know that I'd spent the last week in Asia with her. Everyone was too busy buzzing about Bryn's new love interest, some Australian actor.

There's a note at the front desk informing me that the band is having a private dinner in the atrium and asking me to join them. I suddenly feel like I'm being led to my execution and after the fifteen-hour trip from Seoul would like nothing more than to shower first, just maybe see them tomorrow. But Mia has her hand on my side. "No, you should go."

"You come, too?" I feel bad asking her. She just played three intensely amazing and crazily well-received concerts in Japan and Korea and then flew halfway around the world and directly into my psychodrama. But all of this will be bearable if she's with me.

"Are you sure?" she asks. "I don't want to intrude."

"Trust me, if anyone's intruding, it's me."

The bellman grabs our stuff to take to our room, and

the concierge leads us across the lobby. The hotel is in an old castle, but it's been taken over with rockers and a bunch of different musicians nod and "hey" me, but I'm too nervous right now to respond. The concierge leads us to a dimly lit atrium. The band's all in there, along with a giant buffet serving a traditional English roast.

Liz turns around first. Things haven't been the same between the two of us since that *Collateral Damage* tour, but the look she gives me now, I don't know how to describe it: Like I'm her biggest disappointment in life, but she tries to rise above it, to tamp it down, to act all casual, like I'm just one of the fans, one of the hangers-on, one of the many people who want something from her that she's not obliged to give. "Adam," she says with a curt nod.

"Liz," I begin cautiously.

"Hey, asshole! Nice of you to join us!" Fitzy's irrepressible voice is both sarcastic and welcoming, like he just can't decide which way to go.

Mike doesn't say anything. He just pretends I don't exist.

And then I feel the brush of Mia's shoulder as she steps out from behind me. "Hi, guys," she says.

Liz's face goes completely blank for a moment. Like she doesn't know who Mia is. Then she looks scared, like she's just seen a ghost. Then my strong, tough, butchy drummer—her lower lip starts to tremble, and then her face crumples. "Mia?" she asks, her voice quavering. "Mia?" she asks louder this time. "Mia!" she says, the tears streaming down her face right before she tackles my girl in a hug.

When she's released her, she holds Mia at arm's length and looks at her and then back at me and then back at Mia. "Mia?" she shouts, both asking and answering her own question. Then she turns to me. And if I'm not forgiven, then at least I'm understood.

The rain keeps up throughout the next day. "Lovely English summer we're having," everyone jokes. It's become my habit to barricade myself at these types of giant festivals, but realizing that this is probably my last one for a while, at least as a participant, I slip inside the grounds, listen to some of the bands on the side stages, catch up with some old friends and acquaintances, and even talk to a couple of rock reporters. I'm careful not to mention the breakup of the band. That'll come out in time, and I'll let everyone else decide how to release this news. I do, however, briefly comment on Bryn's and my split, which is all over the tabloids anyhow. Asked about my new mystery woman, I simply say "no comment." I know this will *all* come out soon enough, and while

I want to spare Mia the circus, I don't care if the whole world knows we're together.

By the time our nine P.M. slot rolls around, the rain has subsided to a soft mist that seems to dance in the late summer twilight. The crowd has long since accepted the slosh. There's mud everywhere and people are rolling around in it like it's Woodstock or something.

Before the set, the band was nervous. Festivals do that to us. A bigger ante than regular concerts, even stadium shows—festivals have exponentially larger crowds, and crowds that include our musician peers. Except tonight, I'm calm. My chips are all cashed out. There's nothing to lose. Or maybe I've already lost it and found it, and whatever else there might be to lose, it's got nothing to do with what's on this stage. Which might explain why I'm having such a good time out here, pounding through our new songs on my old Les Paul Junior, another piece of history brought back from the dead. Liz did a double take when she saw me pull it out of its old case. "I thought you got rid of that thing," she'd said.

"Yeah, me too," I'd replied, tossing off a private smile at Mia.

We race through the new album and then throw in some bones from *Collateral Damage* and before I know it, we're almost at the end of the set. I look down at the set list that's duct-taped to the front of the stage.

Scrawled there in Liz's block lettering is the last song before we leave for the inevitable encore. "Animate." Our anthem, our old producer Gus Allen, called it. The angstiest screed on *Collateral Damage*, critics called it. Probably our biggest hit of all. It's a huge crowd-pleaser on tours because of the chorus, which audiences love to chant.

It's also one of the few songs we've ever done with any kind of production, a strings section of violins right at the top of the recorded track, though we don't have those for the live version. So as we launch into it, it's not that rolling howl of the crowd's excitement that I hear, but the sound of her cello playing in my head. For a second, I have this vision of just the two of us in some anonymous hotel room somewhere dickering around, her on her cello, me on my guitar, playing this song I wrote for her. And shit, if that doesn't make me so damn happy.

I sing the song with all I've got. Then we get to the chorus: *Hate me. Devastate me. Annihilate me. Re-create me. Re-create me. Won't you, won't you, won't you re-create me.*

On the album, the chorus is repeated over and over, a rasp of fury and loss, and it's become a thing during shows for me to stop singing and turn the mic out toward the audience and let them take over. So I turn the mic toward the fields, and the crowd just goes insane, singing my song, chanting my plea.

I leave them at it and I take a little walk around the stage. The rest of the band sees what's going on so they just keep repping the chorus. When I get closer to the side of the stage, I see her there, where she always felt most comfortable, though for the foreseeable future, she'll be the one out here in the spotlight, and I'll be the one in the wings, and that feels right, too.

The audience keeps singing, keeps making my case, and I just keep strumming until I get close enough to see her eyes. And then I start singing the chorus. Right to her. And she smiles at me, and it's like we're the only two people out here, the only ones who know what's happening. Which is that this song we're all singing together is being rewritten. It's no longer an angry plea shouted to the void. Right here, on this stage, in front of eighty thousand people, it's becoming something else.

This is our new vow.

ACKNOWLEDGMENTS

It is customary in these types of things for writers to thank their editors and agents separately. But when I think of my writing career, I often imagine myself flanked by my editor, Julie Strauss-Gabel, and my agent, Sarah Burnes. These two fiercely intelligent book warriors are both so integral to the creation and guidance of my work that it's hard to separate them. Sarah advises, advocates, and helps me keep things in perspective. Julie's greatest gift is that she gives me the key to unlock my stories. The two of them are my twin pillars.

But, as the saying goes, it takes a village. And in Julie's case, that village consists of many, many dedicated people at the Penguin Young Readers Group. I will save some trees and not list them all but suffice it to say, there are dozens of people in the sales, marketing, publicity, design, online, and production departments to whom I am deeply—and daily—grateful. Shout-outs must go to Don Weisberg, Lauri Hornik, Lisa Yoskowitz, and Allison Verost, who is equal parts publicist, therapist, and friend.

Sarah's village at The Gernert Company includes Rebecca Gardner, Logan Garrison, Will Roberts, and the formidable Courtney Gatewood, who, for someone bent on world domination, is remarkably nice.

Thank you to Alisa Weilerstein, for inspiring me, as well as giving up some of her precious free time to help me understand the career trajectory for a young professional cellist. Thank you Lynn Eastes, trauma coordinator at OHSU, for offering insights into what Mia's recovery and rehabilitation process might look like. Thank you to Sean Smith for an insider's view into the film industry (and a million other things). Anything I got right in regard to these details is because of these people. Anything I got wrong is because of me.

Thank you to the Edna St. Vincent Millay Society for the generous use of one of my all-time favorite sonnets, "Love is not all: it is not meat nor drink." Many of Edna St. Vincent Millay's poems are incredibly romantic and yet still kind of edgy all these years later. I only included the second half of this sonnet in the book; you should all go look up the full sonnet.

Thank you to my readers at all stages: Jana Banin, Tamara Glenny, Marjorie Ingall, Tamar Schamhart, and Courtney Sheinmel for just the right mix of encouragement and critique.

Thank you to my other village—my neighborhood community—for pitching in with my kids and generally having my back. Isabel Kyriacou and Gretchen Sonju, I am forever in your debt!

Thank you to the entire Christie Family for their enduring grace and generosity.

Thank you to Greg and Diane Rios for continuing on this journey with us.

Thank you to my family, the Formans, Schamharts, and Tuckers, for your cheerleading and cheer. Extra thanks to my sister for hand-selling my books to half the population of Seattle.

Thank you to my daughters: Denbele, who arrived in our family about midway through the writing of this book, and if she ever thought it was weird that her new mom occasionally seemed to channel an angsty twenty-one-year-old guy, never let that dent her ebullience. And to Willa, who inadvertently supplied me with so many of the book's fictional band/movie/character names in a way that only a four/five-year-old can. I should probably raise your allowance.

Thank you to my husband, Nick, for your not-so-gentle critiques that always force me to up my game. For your sublime playlists that bring music into my life (and books). For supplying me with all the little band details. And for being the reason I can't seem to stop writing love stories about guitar players.

And finally, thank you to the booksellers, librarians, teachers, and bloggers. For helping books take flight.